Spanish Crush

Elena was a little embarrassed to be hunting Miguel down at work, but also secretly excited. She could picture him looking gorgeous in his bellhop uniform, his tan skin set against the crisp white cotton. She would be poised, striding up to him with the grace of a dancer. "Hello." He'd beam. "I didn't think I'd see you again so soon. What a wonderful surprise." *Elena, you're hopeless,* she thought.

Elena followed Jenna through the canopied front entrance and into the gleaming lobby. They stood beneath a crystal chandelier, its light bouncing off the rosy marble floor. The windows stretched up tall and arcing to graze the ceiling. The molding at the top of the ceiling looked like cake frosting. When Elena glanced over her shoulder, she felt the eyes of the concierge burning into them. She suddenly felt out of place and antsy to leave.

Elena grabbed Jenna's hand and steered her back to the front of the lobby.

"He's obviously not here," she whispered, turning her head to look at Jenna. "That guy behind the desk is giving me the creeps and—" Before she could finish her sentence she felt herself smack into someone. When she turned her head, she found herself staring directly into Miguel's eyes. They were inches from her own. For a split second she thought, *If this boy ever kissed me, this is what it would feel like the moment before our lips touched....*

S.A.S.S.
STUDENTS ACROSS THE SEVEN SEAS

Spain or Shine

Michelle Jellen

speak

An Imprint of Penguin Group (USA) Inc.

To my parents, for their love and support. Thanks for encouraging me to have an adventure in Europe and for helping me get there.

SPEAK
Published by the Penguin Group
Penguin Group (USA) Inc.,
345 Hudson Street, New York, New York 10014, U.S.A.
Penguin Group (Canada), 90 Eglinton Avenue East, Suite 700, Toronto, Ontario, Canada M4P 2Y3
(a division of Pearson Penguin Canada Inc.)
Penguin Books Ltd, 80 Strand, London WC2R 0RL, England
Penguin Ireland, 25 St Stephen's Green, Dublin 2, Ireland
(a division of Penguin Books Ltd)
Penguin Group (Australia), 250 Camberwell Road, Camberwell, Victoria 3124, Australia
(a division of Pearson Australia Group Pty Ltd)
Penguin Books India Pvt Ltd, 11 Community Centre, Panchsheel Park,
New Delhi - 110 017, India
Penguin Group (NZ), Cnr Airborne and Rosedale Roads, Albany, Auckland 1310,
New Zealand (a division of Pearson New Zealand Ltd)
Penguin Books (South Africa) (Pty) Ltd, 24 Sturdee Avenue, Rosebank, Johannesburg 2196,
South Africa

Registered Offices: Penguin Books Ltd, 80 Strand, London WC2R 0RL, England

Published by Speak, an imprint of Penguin Group (USA) Inc., 2005

5 7 9 10 8 6 4

Copyright © Michelle Jellen, 2005
All rights reserved
Interior art and design by Jeanine Henderson. Text set in Imago Book.

LIBRARY OF CONGRESS CATALOGING-IN-PUBLICATION DATA

Jellen, Michelle.
Spain or shine / by Michelle Jellen.
p. cm. – (S.A.S.S.: Students Across the Seven Seas)
Summary: Overshadowed at home by her over-achieving siblings, sixteen-year-old Elena
Holloway spends a semester in Spain, where she explores her talents in a theater class and tries
to attract the attention of a handsome boy.
ISBN 978-0-14-240368-6 (pbk.)
[1. Self-confidence—Fiction. 2. Foreign study—Fiction. 3. Theater—Fiction. 4. Schools—Fiction.
5. Spain—Fiction.] I. Title. II. Series.
PZ7.J392Spa 2005 [Fic]—dc22 2005043445

Printed in the United States of America

Spain or Shine

Elena's San Sebastián

Bay of
Biscay

Monte Urgull

Parte Vieja

Plaza de la Constitución

Playa de Zurriola

Alameda del Boulevard

Playa de la Concha

Hotel María Cristina

Río Urumea

Application for the Students Across the Seven Seas
Study Abroad Program

Name: Elena Holloway
Age: 16
High School: Mountain Vista High School
Hometown: San Jose, California
Preferred Study Abroad Destination: San Sebastián, Spain

1. Why are you interested in traveling abroad next year?

Answer: I'm interested in further developing my Spanish-speaking skills and I hope that exploring my grandparents' birth country will give me a better understanding of my heritage, as well as an appreciation for other cultures.

(Truth: Studying abroad is one of the only things the overachievers in my family haven't already laid claim to. This is my chance to do something exciting and different.)

2. How will studying abroad further develop your talents and interests?

Answer: The insights I gather while living in a foreign country will enrich the quality of characters and themes in my playwriting.

(Truth: I might actually meet people who don't already know me as "that other Holloway girl.")

3. Describe your extracurricular activities.

Answer: Staff writer for <u>Theater Beat</u> (my school paper), Social Service Club member, Junior Filmmakers Society member

(Truth: I spend most of my time either hanging out with my best friend Claire or daydreaming about the boys I'm going to meet in Spain.)

4. Is there anything else you feel we should know about you?

Answer: My passion for theater and Spanish culture make me an asset to the academic program. My desire to meet new people makes me an ideal S.A.S.S. program participant.

(Truth: I plan on spending every spare moment lounging on the beach and taking in the Spanish nightlife.)

Chapter One

"Maybe I shouldn't go," Elena said, gawking at the clothes splayed out across her bed. She still hadn't decided what to pack, and she was leaving for Spain the next morning.

"Oh no, don't you dare chicken out now," her best friend, Claire, said, plunking down on the only corner of the bed not covered in tank tops and skirts. "You're going to have a blast. At least one of us should have a good time this fall."

"I still can't believe you're not coming."

"And all because of a C in history," Claire groaned. "How could I not qualify for the program? It's so embarrassing."

"Stop beating yourself up about it. You'll have other

chances to go to Europe." Elena began rooting in the closet for her pink flip-flops. "Besides, you're not the one who's going to miss homecoming and all the good summer gossip." She lobbed the flip-flops at the bed. One of them made it, but the other landed on her desk.

"I guess," Claire sulked. "I was really excited about the play production class. Your sister's friend said the teacher devotes entire classes to real method acting techniques."

"Claire, you've been in every school and community play for the last three years. Besides, you'll learn all those things in college."

"Which is, like, a million years from now." She threw her hands in the air. "Oh, don't listen to me. I'm just jealous that you're taking my ideal class without me. Acting, playwriting, and directing all in one class—it's perfect." She shook her head slowly. "You could never get all that here."

Elena wrapped an arm around her friend. "Someday when you're a famous actress and I'm a Tony-winning playwright, we'll laugh about all of this, okay?"

Elena waved at the mess on her bed. "Will you help me with this?" she asked as a way of distracting Claire. "You're better at putting outfits together than me."

Claire started picking through the pile, embracing her new role as fashion consultant. "Definitely bring this. I've heard they wear a ton of black in Europe," she said, handing Elena a black tank top.

As Elena tossed the shirt into her suitcase and tried to think of more ways to distract Claire, her sister, Gwen, walked into their shared bedroom.

"How's it going?" Gwen asked. She was wearing running shorts and a sweat-ringed T-shirt. Although her face was flushed and free of makeup, she still managed to look gorgeous, as always.

"It's going okay," Elena answered.

"Want me to help you organize?" Gwen leaned over Elena's shoulder and peered down at the heap of clothes.

"That'd probably be a good idea."

Gwen cleared out the pile inside the suitcase and began rolling shirts into tight tubes and lining the bottom of the suitcase with them.

"What are you doing?" Claire asked, motioning toward one of the rolled shirts.

"You can pack more this way," Gwen explained.

Elena and Claire took over rolling clothes after Gwen had demonstrated with a few T-shirts.

"So, how do you feel about all this, Lanie?" Gwen parked on the edge of her bed and began loosening the laces of her running shoes.

"Nervous," Elena said.

"Nervous and excited, though?"

"Yeah. But mostly nervous."

Gwen slipped her shoes off, kicking them toward her

closet. "Well, I think it's really cool that you're following through with this."

"Yeah, it is sort of unlike me, isn't it?" Elena said.

"I'm being serious," Gwen said. "It's just that you have all these great ideas and...like, remember the time you were going to run for class secretary and you made half the posters and then just dropped the whole thing because you were sure you couldn't beat Claudia Kauffman?"

"I know. I'm not great at follow-through."

"I'm just saying I think this trip is going to be amazing." Elena hadn't realized how much she valued Gwen's approval until she'd actually heard the words.

"Melanie met these two girls last year in Spain who were also in the S.A.S.S. program," Gwen continued, "and they're, like, two of her best friends now. You're going to meet so many cool people." Gwen's friend, Melanie, was the one who had introduced Elena and Claire to the whole idea of the S.A.S.S. program in San Sebastián.

"I hope so," Elena said as she rolled a shirt. The roll wasn't nearly as small and perfect as Gwen's had been.

They were interrupted by the sharp smack of the front door slamming shut, followed by a clatter in the hallway. Elena recognized the sounds of her fourteen-year-old-brother, Caleb, dumping his football equipment next to the door. Caleb's heavy footsteps thumped across the foyer.

Elena's mom's voice boomed from the kitchen. "Caleb, you are not allowed into the living room until you take off your dirty cleats. And don't leave them in the hall—someone will trip over them and break their neck!" According to Elena's mom, they were all perpetually in danger of breaking their necks or poking their eyes out.

"Relax, Mom, I'm going to take a shower," Caleb called.

"Oh no, he isn't." Gwen leaped off the bed and flew toward the bathroom across the hall. Elena could hear Gwen and Caleb scrambling toward the bathroom door.

"I should go first. You never leave any hot water," Gwen hollered as she slipped inside the bathroom and swung the door shut before Caleb could pry his way in. Caleb pounded on the bathroom door.

"What a madhouse." Elena shut her door in an attempt to seal out some of the racket. "So, what am I forgetting? Do you think I need a raincoat?"

"Forget the raincoat. This is all you really need," Claire said, holding up a turquoise bikini splashed with tiny pink hearts. Elena laughed, snatching the dangling bikini from Claire's hand and dropping it into her suitcase. The bikini was Elena's secret weapon. Elena had seen it in a magazine in May and hunted it down through phone calls and Internet searches. She'd never wanted a single piece of clothing so much in her life. Even with limbs as skinny and pale as birch branches, Elena thought she looked pretty good in the bikini. She felt like the best version of herself.

Outside the bedroom window darkness painted the sky. That was Elena's cue to usher Claire toward the door. She

walked Claire out to the front porch, and they stood for a moment in the warm, late August air, listening to the silence.

"It's only three and a half months," Claire said finally, waving her hand as if that amount of time was so small she could shoo it away like a fly.

"That's nothin'." Elena hugged her friend. She couldn't remember a time when they hadn't started the school year together.

"See ya," Claire said over her shoulder as she stepped out toward the street.

"See ya," Elena echoed.

Over the years they'd perfected the art of saying goodbye without making it sound sad or significant. Elena watched Claire's silhouette melt into the shadows. Her heart sank into her chest, and self-doubt began to seep in. It felt impossible to do this thing on her own, but this was her opportunity to do something brave and cool that none of the overachievers in her family had already done. In Spain she would have the chance to be something other than another one of the Holloway kids or Claire's best friend. She could just be Elena, whoever that was.

As soon as Elena stepped through the front door she heard her mom calling everyone to dinner. Elena ambled through the door to the kitchen and found her mom, Carla, looking all businesslike in a skirt, a silk blouse, and ostrich-skin heels. Her hands, however, were incongruously sheathed in oven mitts. She flew across the kitchen turning off buzzers, lifting plates, and filling glasses.

Gwen stood at the counter, making a salad. Elena grabbed a carrot slice and Gwen smacked her hand playfully.

"Mom, Elena stole a carrot," Gwen whined, but then stuck a carrot slice into her own mouth and winked at Elena.

"Better carrots than cupcakes," her mom answered in her weary half-listening voice.

Elena and Gwen giggled. "Whatever that means," Gwen muttered to Elena.

On her way toward the table Elena stepped over Caleb, who was sprawled out on the kitchen floor in his sweaty football clothes reading a comic book. This was apparently the compromise he and their mom had come to regarding her demand that he not go into the living room in his dirty practice jersey.

"All right, everyone take a seat," her mom said, carrying a piping dish of lasagna over to the counter.

Caleb clicked over to the table, leaving a trail of grass-threaded dirt clumps from his cleats. Elena joined him, followed by Gwen and their mom.

"So, I did an Internet search today on the top schools in the nation," Gwen said as soon as they began eating.

Caleb groaned. "God, can we for once not talk about colleges? That's all I ever hear about in this house." He speared a hunk of lasagna with his fork.

Elena silently agreed with Caleb. The pressure of college looming caused Elena's family to spend a lot of time lately

talking about how to be exceptional. Elena was just trying to get through her classes with good grades, let alone exceptional ones. But silently, she acknowledged that this trip to Spain was her chance to be exceptional in a different way. She was going to pursue this thing, playwriting and production, that she might possibly excel at in a way her other siblings never could. Or she could fall flat on her face.

Caleb and Gwen continued to argue while their mom tried several times to interrupt with a cheerful story about a recent home sale. She gave up when the phone rang. Moments later the front door slammed, and Elena's oldest sibling, Jeremy, who was home from college for the summer, sauntered into the kitchen.

"Hey, what's for dinner? I'm starving," he said.

Elena took another bite of lasagna. She was usually the quiet one at the table. In the Holloway house, whoever spoke loudest won, and unfortunately Elena had been born with a quiet set of pipes.

Gwen had finished her salad and was now eating tiny little nibbles of lasagna. She was constantly watching her weight, although Elena honestly had trouble finding any weight on her that needed watching.

"Want mine?" Elena whispered, offering her untouched salad to Gwen while her mom was talking on the phone. Gwen nodded and quickly swapped bowls with Elena.

Elena's mom hung up the phone and sighed. "I have to take some clients out to look at houses. This is the only time they can go." She walked over and kissed the top of Elena's head. "I'm sorry your dad and I can't be with you more on your last night, kiddo."

"It's okay, Mom."

"Well, he'll be home soon. Do you need any help packing before I go?"

"Don't worry about it. Gwen's helping me."

Elena's mom scurried out the door, and Gwen and Caleb helped Elena carry the dishes to the sink. The dinner dishes were her designated daily chore.

Jeremy spooned lukewarm lasagna onto a plate as Caleb and Gwen left the kitchen.

"What's up, Lanie?" Jeremy asked, sitting at the breakfast bar to eat.

"Not much, just need to finish packing," she answered.

"Does it feel weird to be going without Claire?" he asked. Since Jeremy had left for college last year he had become much more interested in her life. Elena found it a bit disconcerting. She figured it was a combination of his growing up a little and actually missing his family.

"Yeah, I'm sort of nervous about going without her. But, to be honest, I also think it'll be good for me to branch out."

"Yeah, you guys *are* together a lot. It just seems funny that you're the one going since she's the drama nerd."

"She's not a nerd," Elena defended.

"I just meant she's the one interested in acting," he explained. She could tell by the lack of sarcasm in his voice

that he was being sincere. "I hadn't pegged you for the actress is all. You seem more like the backstage type."

"I'm definitely not an actress," she confirmed, scraping off the dinner plates. "The course is play production. It's a little bit of everything: acting, playwriting, directing."

"Playwriting." He eyed her. "The next best thing to screenwriting, huh?" Jeremy shared Elena's love of movies and was one of the few people, along with Claire, who knew about her secret dream of becoming a famous screenwriter/director.

Elena nodded.

"That's cool," Jeremy said. "I bet you'll be good at it."

"I don't know. We'll see," she said. But then she added, "I really hope so."

Elena heard the front door open. Moments later her dad came strolling into the kitchen.

"Hey, guys, what's for dinner?"

"Lasagna," Elena told him, pointing with a soapy finger.

"Elena, you shouldn't be doing dishes on your last night. Leave those. I'll get to them later. Or maybe Jeremy can offer his services." Her dad raised an eyebrow at Jeremy.

Jeremy set his empty plate next to the sink. "All right, I'll do them tomorrow morning," he sighed.

"Thanks, Dad." Elena smiled at him and turned the water off. She was already beginning to feel a little bit special.

As she was drying her hands she realized that tomorrow, while Jeremy was washing dishes, she would be thirty thousand feet up, soaring toward a foreign country.

• • •

Elena woke before dawn and tiptoed into the bathroom. She'd showered the night before so she could sleep as late as possible, which wasn't very late at all. After washing her face and drying it with a towel, she slid a comb through her hair. Elena's wavy hair was a warm shade of brown. She pulled it into a low ponytail, smeared her lips with strawberry gloss, and gave her colorless cheeks a pinch. That was about as good as it was going to get at four thirty in the morning.

Both of her parents had gotten up to take her to the airport. When they finished checking her in, Elena spotted a woman in her forties holding up a laminated sign for the International School, or I.S. She was sure this was the chaperone she'd been told would be accompanying the students from Northern California to San Sebastián. The chaperone wore too-high-waisted khaki shorts in a material that stretched tight and shiny across a pooch of belly. Elena watched as she greeted several of the students who had already managed to shake their parents. When the students approached her, she beamed, welcoming them in a voice that rose and fell like a song. She was entirely too perky for six A.M. Elena guessed she was the type of woman who went to Disneyland every year for her vacation—even though she was at least forty-five—and had a compilation of collector's plates ordered from TV infomercials.

Although Elena had pointed out the chaperone to her

parents and explained that she could take it from here, her mom kept finding one last thing to say. She wondered if her mom was ever going to let her go.

"Be sure to call us as soon as you land," she said.

"Mom, it's going to be, like, three in the morning here when I get to San Sebastián."

"I don't care. You just use the calling card I gave you." She roped Elena in for the third hug in five minutes. "And remember to stick with the group. Don't dawdle in the airport, or you might get lost. Pay attention to the chaperone." Elena was so used to these pleas from her mother to stay focused that she just tuned them out.

When her mom pulled back, pools were forming in her eyes. That was Elena's cue. If her mom started to cry, she'd never get out of there.

"She'll be fine, Carla," her dad said softly.

"I know." Elena's mother's tears were on the verge of spilling now. "Try and visit your great-aunt Elena and your cousins when you're there. They're your family. Nothing's more important than family; remember that."

"I want to visit them, Mom. I just don't know for sure if I'll have time. I already told you that." She glanced over at the lady in the khaki shorts. "Now I really have to go," she said, giving both of her parents a quick hug and looping her backpack strap over her shoulder. Her mom thrust a bag into her hand as she headed toward Khaki Shorts.

"So you don't get bored on the plane," she whispered.

Elena approached Khaki Shorts and gave her name.

"Here you are," Khaki Shorts said after scanning her list. "Elena Holloway. Welcome. My name is Brenda. Have you ever been to Spain, Elena?"

"Nopè. Never left the country," Elena returned, hoping she sounded casual.

"Well, this will be exciting. Okay, Elena, line up with the rest of the group. It's time to go through security." The way she kept using Elena's name felt forced. It was as though someone had taught her that repeating the kids' names would make her sound more trustworthy.

Elena walked up to the group of students who were forming a line and inserted herself between a girl in jeans and a tank top and a boy wearing a black baseball hat pulled down low on his forehead. She didn't feel too out of place yet. But she knew that would change once they got to Spain. The program she would be attending in San Sebastián was situated on a local high school campus, so she knew she would be seeing lots of Spanish people on and off of school grounds. Plus, even though all the students in the International School were English speakers, they would be coming from all over the United States, as well as England, Ireland, and even as far away as Australia. She decided to enjoy the comfort of being with people who dressed and spoke like her friends for the short time it lasted.

• • •

The plane was nearly full when Elena found her seat next to a man in a charcoal business suit. She squeezed past his knees and slid into her window seat. In order to get a deal on prices the school had been unable to seat the students together on the plane. Brenda had apologized profusely for this, but Elena was privately glad since she was really too nervous about the upcoming trip to make small talk with a stranger. The man sitting next to her, scowling at a stack of papers, didn't look like one for chatter.

She peered through the oval window at the streaks of red dawn rippling through the fog-sodden sky. Looking out over the bay made her feel homesick already, so she closed the window shade and dug into the plastic bag her mom had given her, pulling the contents onto her knees. Inside the bag she found three magazines, a guidebook on Spain, a pack of gum, candy, earplugs, and eye shades.

Elena was probably the least likely one of her siblings to go on a journey like this, but she was hoping to surprise everyone with her bravery. She set the plastic bag down, slipped her iPod out of the front pouch of her backpack, and cued up a Strokes song Caleb had downloaded for her. Maybe a little irreverent rock would slam some courage into her veins. A surge of frenetic drums blended with the rumble of the plane's engine. The cabin began to jostle as the plane rolled down the runway. She closed her eyes, gripped the armrests, and thought, *Here goes nothin'.*

Chapter Two

The first part of San Sebastián Elena spotted from the air was the shell-shaped beach, Playa de la Concha. It was a thin ribbon of sand laid in a half circle, with a dab of green land tucked in the mouth of the bay that opened out to sea. She'd read about this famous beach during the long plane ride from San Francisco to Madrid. The tour book her mom gave her explained that Playa de la Concha was a magnet for the Spanish and French alike due to its location at the northern tip of Spain, only a skip away from the French border. She imagined herself stretched out on the sand, lulled by the sound of water and wind. This was what she'd been

dreaming about for months, and now she was actually here.

Elena craned her neck for a better view of the beach below. She tried to be careful not to wake the boy next to the window who'd fallen asleep with his black baseball hat pulled down over his eyes. She wished she could fall asleep sitting up like that. Her muscles were twitching, she was so exhausted. She leaned forward a little closer to the window, but her forearm slipped and bumped into the sleeping guy's arm. He mumbled and opened his eyes.

"Sorry," she said, shrinking back in her seat. He waved off her apology affably and rubbed his eyes.

"Man, I can't wait to get out there," he nodded toward the view from the window. "Doesn't it look awesome from up here?" He looked at her expectantly.

"Awesome," she said.

He bobbed his head as if she'd just said something profound. "Hey, I recognize you from the airport in San Francisco. You're from California, too, huh?" He pushed his hat up slightly and peered out from beneath its brim.

"Yeah. I live in San Jose," she said.

"Cool. I'm from Santa Cruz."

It didn't surprise her that this guy was from a beach town. He wore a pale blue Hurley sweatshirt, and clumps of sea-crisped hair poked out from beneath his hat like dry yellow grass. He looked like the guys at her high school who would drive thirty minutes or more every weekend in search of the perfect wave. He wasn't the kind of guy she normally hung out with, but the sight of him was familiar, and right now anything familiar was welcome.

"I'm Alex," he said.

"Elena. Nice to meet you."

"Right on," he said, giving her a half nod, then glancing back at the window. "I can't wait to ride those waves."

"You're a surfer?" she asked, though she was pretty sure she knew the answer.

"Yep. That's what I'm here for."

"To surf?"

"Yeah. Well, not just to surf. I mean, I can do that at home, right? The surf in San Sebastián's going to be gnarly, but I'm really stoked about exploring a foreign country. My family's big on travel. This summer my older brother Keith and I traveled all over California and Colorado—camping, hiking, climbing, that kind of stuff," he explained. "What about you? Do you travel a lot?"

Before Elena could tell Alex that her family had hardly left the Bay area, they were interrupted by the flight attendant announcing that they would be landing soon. Elena stole another glance at Alex. He was definitely cute, in a scruffy-beach-bum sort of way. But she was on the lookout for something else completely. She'd known boys like Alex all her life. She wanted to meet someone exotic. And an accent wouldn't hurt. Accents were always sexy.

"So, dorm or family?" he asked once the flight attendant had clicked off the speaker.

"Excuse me?"

"We were supposed to choose between staying in the dorms, or with a host family? Which one did you pick?"

"Oh, right. I chose the host family, but to be honest, right now I'm not so sure about that decision. My Spanish is pretty lame, and I'm going to be living with strangers. I just have no idea what to expect." Her stomach fluttered at the thought of meeting her host family at the airport. These would be the people she would live with, eat with, and share a bathroom with for the next three months. Elena said a silent prayer to whoever might be listening to miraculously grant her an out-going personality and master Spanish-speaking skills.

"No worries. I chose a host family, too."

"You did?"

"Yeah. It's definitely the way to go. It's the only way to get a real insider's view of Spain. I've heard that living with locals forces you to speak Spanish sooner and eat more local food and stuff."

Elena appreciated that this guy, Alex, was trying to pump her up, but he was just emphasizing all the reasons she was nervous to begin with. She'd already gotten lost during the stopover in Madrid. They'd had a long layover, and some of the kids had gone into the airport shops. She'd wandered over to a scarf store, but had forgotten to notice the time and couldn't remember the connecting gate. After about ten excruciatingly long minutes she figured out which gate was hers on the monitor, but it had been a reminder that she needed to be more responsible during her time in Spain. After those few minutes alone in a foreign airport she'd vowed to herself that things would be different here. She'd pay attention and stop daydreaming.

The little puddle jumper they'd boarded in Madrid touched down on the tarmac with several screechy bumps. This was it; Elena had arrived. As soon as the plane stopped rolling and people began standing up and gathering their things, Brenda rushed to the front of the aisle.

"All righty, kids. Stick with me on the way out. We're going to do a head count as soon as we get off the plane." Her eyes darted around the plane's interior. She seemed to be doing her own silent head count now as if she might lose someone on an airplane the size of a narrow living room.

"Dude, this chick makes me feel like I'm on a kindergarten field trip." Alex snickered, zipping up his backpack.

"I know," Elena ventured. "She'd probably insist on coming into the bathroom with me."

"Totally." A laugh slid from the back of his throat, slow and thick as honey. "Then she'd do a head count to make sure you didn't get lost on the way back to your seat."

She felt a pang of guilt for mocking Brenda. Though she was annoyingly perky and needlessly protective, Elena was secretly glad she was there to lead the way. She seemed to know her way around airports, and her Spanish was perfect. But she was such an easy target. Why was it that one of the quickest ways to bond with another teenager was to make

fun of a dorky adult? Elena decided to give herself a break and chalk this one up to social survival.

Brenda corralled the students together once they were inside the airport.

"Settle down, everyone," she hollered. Elena noticed Brenda's once neatly pressed khaki shorts were now wrinkled, particularly where they hugged her midsection. She looked as rumpled and tired as Elena felt. Elena had managed to log a few restless hours of sleep on the first flight, although sleep might have been too generous a term. It was more like a light nap. She rubbed at the knot that had tightened in her neck. She felt as if she could go to sleep forever.

"Okay, as you know, you were each given the choice to either room in the campus dorm, or stay with a host family while you're here in San Sebastián," Brenda continued, once the students had hushed. "If you chose the dorm option, you'll stay here with me. If you're meeting with a family, please go check in with Pierce." She pointed to a gangly redhead. He wore a navy blue collared shirt with the International School emblem stitched over his heart. It was the same type of shirt Brenda had tucked into her shorts.

Elena walked with Alex and two others toward Pierce. He was encircled by couples and their kids, whom Elena took to be the host families. Elena had never really understood the phrase "alone in a crowd" before. But as she stood there, surrounded by students and Spanish families, she'd never felt so alone. Normally Gwen, the outgoing one, would step forward and take control of the situation. Or she could always count on her brothers to tell a joke to lighten the tension. This was the first time that she didn't have one of her siblings or Claire with her for support. She couldn't help feeling as if she could get swept away with the sea of strangers and no one would even notice.

By the time it was Elena's turn to give her name there were only two Spanish people, a woman and a girl, left standing beside Pierce. The woman was built like a dancer, and the girl, clearly her daughter, was a miniature replica of the woman. This was obviously her host family, but Pierce insisted Elena give her name anyway.

"Those are the rules," he asserted, without even cracking a smile. Was this guy for real?

"Holloway," she said, "Elena Holloway."

He scanned his list. "Elena Holloway." He drew a check mark next to her name. "Elena, I'd like to introduce you to Señora Cruz and her daughter, Alita." Then he turned to Señora Cruz and said in elegantly accented Spanish, *"Es un placer presentarle la Señorita Holloway."* Show off.

The woman stepped closer and offered a slender hand decorated with silver rings. *"Es un placer conocerle,"* she said, shaking Elena's hand gently. *"Bienvenido."*

"Gracias," Elena returned in a voice that seemed to evaporate into the air around her. She was aware that the accent she'd learned in school was different from the one spoken in

Spain. Señora Cruz pronounced her *s* sounds lightly, with the hint of a lisp. It sounded soft and graceful.

The young girl marched forward, jutting her hand out and grinning.

"Hi, my name is Alita." Her English was clear and molded only by a faint accent. She smiled proudly, seeming to know how good she sounded. "Pleased to meet you." As Elena shook her hand, she wondered how old the girl was. She looked about eight, but she seemed too sure of herself. Elena guessed her small stature made her appear younger than she actually was.

"Alita is excited to practice her English," Señora Cruz explained, wrapping an arm around Alita's shoulders. Elena was relieved they were all speaking English now.

Pierce said good-bye and walked over to Brenda, leaving Elena alone with her pretend family. She followed them out to their Fiat and watched as bird-thin Señora Cruz somehow managed to heave Elena's luggage into a trunk the size of a pocket and squeeze the lid shut.

"Now we go home," Señora Cruz said, smoothing down the front of her black top and pants. It looked as though Claire's theory about Europeans wearing a lot of black wasn't far off the mark.

Elena squished herself into the backseat and zoned out as the car bumped down the road headed for town. Alita turned around in front, kneeling in the scoop of her seat, and began firing questions at Elena.

"Where do you live?" she quizzed, her chin propped on the headrest of her seat. She wasn't wearing a seat belt.

"California."

"In Hollywood?" Her face lit up.

"No," Elena said, choking on a giggle that came out as a broken cough. "Closer to San Francisco, actually."

Alita nodded eagerly. "San Francisco has the Golden Gate Bridge, yes?"

"Yes," Elena answered, stifling a yawn.

"I know everything about America."

Señora Cruz said something in Spanish Elena didn't understand, which caused Alita to turn forward and sit down in her seat.

"Alita is excited to have you living with us for the semester," Señora Cruz offered seemingly as an apology for her daughter's persistent chatter. "Alita is very good with language. Her teacher says she knows more English words than any other ten-year-old at school."

"Oh. That's impressive." Elena really didn't mind Alita's questions. If only she could get some sleep first.

They drove along a road cut into the hills. On one side of the car stood a wall of land, but on the other side Elena could see the ocean. The town shimmered in the distance, nestled in the crook of two green mountains that rose up on either side. It looked like a fairy-tale city from afar.

Finally Señora Cruz pulled the car over to the curb in front of an apartment building. Elena helped Señora Cruz get her

bags out of the trunk, then stood for a moment inhaling air so salty she could taste it on her tongue. She gazed down the long, crooked road that slanted toward the ocean. Elena was sure the sunlight fell differently here, washing everything in a warm golden light. She traced the tops of the tall buildings made of stone and stucco that had been baked into shades of brown, gold, and peach after centuries under the sun's rays. These buildings were older than any she'd seen at home. In California, a building was considered historic if it had been built before the 1950s. The buildings here were so timeless they didn't seem like man-made structures at all. It was as if they'd grown gradually up from the earth like trees.

Señor Cruz greeted them at the curb in fine wool pants and a neatly pressed cotton shirt. *"Hola,"* he said, dipping into a neat little bow. Although he was a small man, his trimmed hair and tailored clothing made his presence much larger. "Spanish men take pride in their appearance," she remembered her mother saying several times as she was growing up, usually when Elena's dad or brothers were looking particularly sloppy.

Señor Cruz stepped in to help Elena carry her bags up the two flights of stairs to their apartment.

The front of their apartment building was surrounded by an ancient stone wall crawling with moss and vines, but the inside of their apartment was spare and clean. The furniture was modern and the walls bright white. The smiling faces that beamed out at her from framed photos and the sun-colored curtains made Elena feel as if this was a happy place to live. Señora Cruz led her through a narrow hallway to the bedroom at the end of the apartment.

"This will be your room," she said. "Make yourself comfortable." Then she left the room and closed the door behind her to give Elena some privacy.

The room wasn't much bigger than a walk-in closet, and it was nearly empty, but it was all hers. She did a little twirl and plopped down on the twin bed that was pushed up against the wall under a window. The only other furniture was a bureau that stood next to the closet. Elena considered hanging her nicer shirts and skirts, but weariness had taken hold. Her whole body felt as if it were made of stone. It was now noon on Sunday in San Sebastián. Elena did some calculating and realized that it was three in the morning back home, so she decided to call her mom a little later. Without even turning down the covers, she flopped onto the pillow, closed her eyes, and slipped into a dreamless sleep.

When Elena awoke, the afternoon sun dangled low in the sky. For a moment she thought she was back in her room at home. She half expected Gwen to come bursting through the door. But when she rolled over and looked through the open window, she could see the red-tiled rooftops of apartment buildings glowing in the orangey-pink sunlight. She remembered she was multiple time zones away from home.

Elena walked out into the main room and found Señora

Cruz in the kitchen chopping vegetables and bouncing along with the flamenco guitar that pumped through an old radio on the counter.

"Hola," Elena said, rubbing her eyes.

"Hola, Elena. Please sit, you must be hungry," Señora Cruz said, pulling out a chair at the kitchen table and offering Elena a plate of fruit and cheese.

"Gracias." Elena nibbled on a piece of Swiss cheese. Even though it had been hours since she'd eaten, she really didn't feel hungry. Her stomach was still on California time.

"Alita and Señor Cruz are at the beach. They didn't want to wake you. You should go into town," Señora Cruz urged. "Or go to the beach. It is easy to find."

Elena hesitated. She'd never explored a foreign city alone before. But the alternative was to stay here and hang out with Señora Cruz. Plus, she was eager to get a glimpse of some of the boutiques she'd read about. So she went back into the bedroom to get her guidebook on Spain, which had a little black-and-white map of San Sebastián in the middle. Señora Cruz showed her how to get to town. Just a couple turns and she would be on the beachfront promenade.

"It will be crowded," Señora Cruz said. "On the weekends, everyone goes to the beach. Only three things people take very seriously here: the ocean, food, and wine." Señora Cruz gave her a playful pat on the shoulder, as if to assure her this would be the extent of her worries during her time in Spain.

Elena made a quick phone call to her mom using her

calling card, then stepped through the front door as Señora Cruz called after her to be back in a couple of hours. Elena made her way toward the center of town. The streets were lined with shops and outdoor cafés topped by colorful signs in two or three languages. She recognized some of the Spanish words, and the familiar American brands, like Coca-Cola, were written in English. But each sign also bore a translation in northern Spain's native Basque language, which looked impossible to pronounce with so many *X*s and strings of consonants lined up next to one another—words like *pinxto* and *etxe*.

Elena had been looking forward to popping into a few shops and doing some browsing, if not actual shopping. But it wasn't as easy as she had imagined it would be. Although the streets were littered with people, most shops and restaurants were dim, their doors shut and locked. She'd heard of the siesta custom, but somehow she had imagined it to be a myth, not something people actually did. She couldn't fathom a national movement in the United States where everyone shut down their businesses in the middle of the day to eat a leisurely lunch and take a nap. It would never happen.

Her confused stomach—which was silent when she actually had food—now growled at her. She'd thought for sure there would be a twenty-four hour McDonald's somewhere, but after ducking down several side streets she found nothing. She decided to stray toward the beach, hoping the sight of the ocean would distract her.

She followed Señora Cruz's directions until she came upon the promenade that overlooked Playa de la Concha. She walked over to the curvy white railing and looked down at the beach below. The tide was rising, but people still lounged on the warm sand, stretched out on beach blankets and huddled under striped canopies. Little kids were splashing, happy and naked, in the gentle waves at the edge of the water. She found a stairway and headed down. At the last stair she leaped onto the beach, sending sprays of sand up into the air. It hit her— she was in Spain.

Elena looked up at the cool green mountains flanking the bay and decided it would be hard to feel stressed or unhappy here. In fact, not a single person seemed to be in a hurry to get somewhere. At home she was constantly surrounded by people rushing from one place to another. Time seemed to unfurl more gently here.

She wondered what Claire was doing now. If she were here, she would probably be splashing in the waves with the kids, daring Elena to loosen up and get her feet wet. In honor of Claire she walked out toward the ocean and dipped her feet in, letting the water climb up to her shins.

After sitting on the beach for a few more minutes while her feet dried, Elena stood up, brushed the sand off her pants, and headed toward the road. On her way back up the Paseo, she passed a small shop that was opening. Elena hustled through, looking for a food aisle. She finally found the snack section, grabbed a cylindrical red paper-wrapped package that appeared to be chocolate-filled cookies, and headed toward the register at the front. On the way, she passed a display of postcards and grabbed three cards with photos of the beach at sunset and placed them on the counter.

"¿Cuánto cuesta?" she asked. A little chill shimmied up her spine; she was using Spanish *in Spain.* But when the woman behind the counter answered her question, the words jumbled together in midair. By the time they reached Elena's ears they were just a tangle of syllables.

"Uh, sorry. How much?" she stammered, a flush of pink spreading up her neck and into her cheeks.

The woman repeated her answer in Spanish, but Elena still didn't understand. Her palms broke out in a sweat.

"Um, do you speak English?" she stammered. *"¿Usted habla inglés?"*

The woman shook her head. A line was beginning to form behind her. Finally, a Spanish teenager stepped forward and acted as a translator.

"Those cost three euro, fifty."

Elena dug through her pink corduroy shoulder bag and fumbled with the money she'd exchanged at the airport. When the woman handed her the postcards and cookies tucked in a thin plastic bag, Elena nodded quickly as a thank-you and jetted out the door. She was so embarrassed that she just wanted to evaporate into the air.

She decided to cut her solo tour short and head back up

the promenade to the apartment. After shuffling up the stairs, she paused at the second-floor landing and swore she heard English being spoken on the other side of the door, followed by ripples of laughter. It seemed odd that the Cruzes would be speaking English among themselves.

When she opened the door, she found four sets of eyes directed at her. Only three of them were familiar.

"Elena, how was your walk?" Señora Cruz asked, standing up to greet her.

"It was nice. You were right about the beach being packed, but it was so beautiful," Elena answered, without taking her eyes off the girl sitting on the couch next to Señor Cruz. She had pale blond hair and golden skin, and she peered up at Elena with wide brown eyes. She might not have been quite as beautiful as Elena's sister, but she probably turned more than a few heads.

"We have a surprise visitor," Señora Cruz said, nodding in the direction of the unfamiliar girl. "This is Jenna."

Jenna stood up and teetered across the room on wedge sandals, hand extended.

"Hi," she said, pumping Elena's hand. "Nice to meet you. Señora Cruz said you're from California. That's awesome. I'm from Phoenix."

"Oh. Cool." Elena had the feeling she was missing something. "Are you staying with the Cruzes, too?" she ventured.

Jenna laughed. "Well, sort of."

"Jenna is in the S.A.S.S. program, just like you, Elena,"

Señora Cruz explained. "She is supposed to stay in the dorms, but there was a problem."

"Some of the toilets in the first-floor bathroom overflowed last night, and a bunch of the rooms got flooded," Jenna piped up, sliding her hand through her glossy hair.

"Gross," Elena said.

"I know. So, when I heard that a family was nice enough to offer to put me up for a couple of nights while they clean up my rank dorm room, I was like, 'Yes, please.'"

Señora Cruz motioned for the girls to take a seat. Jenna flopped back on the couch while Elena chose an empty leather chair across the room. Elena was intrigued and a little bit awed by how breezily this girl responded to such a big change in plans upon arriving in Spain. It was inspiring.

Alita came in from the kitchen with a bottle of wine. She set it down in front of her mom, who poured small glasses for the girls and regular ones for herself and Señor Cruz.

"This is famous wine of Basque country," Señor Cruz said, propping the bottle on his forearm like a waiter in a fancy restaurant so the girls could inspect the label.

"Uh, how do you pronounce that?" Jenna asked skeptically, eyeing Elena. Elena was glad Jenna asked; she was wondering the same thing.

"Txakoli," Señor Cruz said easily.

"Cha-co-ly," they repeated.

"Bueno," Señora Cruz proclaimed, clapping her hands. "Your first Basque word."

"Salud," Señor Cruz said, raising his glass up. *"Salud,"* Jenna repeated, clinking her glass up against Elena's. She gave Elena a wink and a look that seemed to say, *Can you believe they're just giving us wine like it's no big deal?*

Elena had heard that Spanish people grew up drinking wine, so she was pretty sure it wasn't out of the ordinary for girls her age to be drinking. She couldn't shake the feeling, however, that she was doing something slightly scandalous. The only time her parents had allowed her to drink was at her cousin's wedding. And here was Señora Cruz pouring a glass for Alita, who was only ten.

Alita stood at the edge of the couch looking like a puppy forced to choose between two bones. Her eyes bounced back and forth between Elena and Jenna, clearly trying to decide which American girl was more interesting. Eventually she seemed to settle on Jenna, planting herself on a cushion next to her on the couch. Elena knew it was petty, but she felt a pinprick of jealousy.

"Jenna and Elena, how were your flights across the Atlantic?" Señora Cruz asked.

"Pretty uneventful," Elena answered, and took a dainty sip of wine. She decided to reserve her story about nearly getting lost in the Madrid airport. She didn't like to reveal that side of herself before she had to.

"Mine, too," Jenna said, leaning back into the couch. "But I almost missed my first plane out of Phoenix."

"Really?" Elena leaned forward with her elbows on her knees.

"Yeah. It's embarrassing," Jenna began, though she looked more amused than embarrassed. "I totally overslept. My mom burst through my door at twenty to seven and starts yelling, 'Get up, Jenna. Get up. We're late.' I didn't even have time to shower. We just hopped in the car. I've never seen my mom drive that fast. She's usually, like, a model citizen on the road."

"It seems you made it here in the end," Señora Cruz noted cheerfully.

"Yep," Jenna took a deep breath and then let out a relieved sigh. "I just barely made the cutoff time for foreign flights."

"Then you get to Spain and your room is flooded," Elena noted, amazed that this girl was holding it together so well. "What an ordeal."

"Tell me about it." Jenna smiled.

"Do you have brothers and sisters?" Alita asked, beaming up at Jenna.

"Well, I have a stepbrother named Danny, but he doesn't live with me, so basically I'm an only child, like you."

As Alita appeared to bask in the idea of being like Jenna in any way, and continued asking questions, Elena shifted in her seat, trying to mask the gurgling sounds coming from her stomach. She was used to eating by six o'clock at home,

but none of the Cruzes seemed to notice how late it was getting. Elena was starting to feel a little light-headed from the wine and her nearly empty stomach.

They finally sat down for dinner at nine thirty. Elena wasn't sure if this was due to Jenna's unexpected arrival, or if this was the norm, but none of the Cruzes acted as if it was out of the ordinary.

"This is a special meal, girls," Señora Cruz began to explain as she lifted the lid off of a skillet. "It is Señor Cruz's favorite."

Señor Cruz beamed. *"Gracias, mi amor,"* he said, as he leaned in to plant a kiss on his wife's pink cheek.

"I believe in America you would call this an omelet," Señora Cruz explained to Elena and Jenna as she spooned out a portion of the omelet thing onto each of their plates. "It is made with *bacalao*, codfish."

Elena mustered a wary thank-you as she eyed the fish omelet. She'd never eaten an omelet for dinner, much less one with fish in it.

"Please tell us more about the program you are starting tomorrow." Señor Cruz sectioned off a large bite of fishy omelet. "Señora Cruz and I are aware that your school is located on the high school campus. Will you be taking classes with Spanish students?"

"The classes are all taught in English, except the conversational Spanish class. That one is obviously a mix of Spanish and English," Elena answered.

"So, are all the students Americans?" Alita asked excitedly.

"No. I'm pretty sure all the girls who applied through S.A.S.S., like me and Jenna, are American. Most of the other kids in the program are from the U.S., too, but there are also some from England, Ireland, and, I think, even Australia."

"They're all from English-speaking countries," Jenna piped in, sliding her fork into her untouched omelet and pulling it out again, leaving four perfect little holes. Elena wondered if she was also unsure about fish in an omelet.

Elena dared to take a bite of her omelet and found it to be surprisingly tasty. It was encouraging. Perhaps trying new things wouldn't be as difficult as she'd thought it would be.

"We should speak in Spanish tonight then," Señor Cruz said. "Elena and Jenna will learn more that way."

The two American girls exchanged glances, and then Jenna shrugged and said, "Why not?" Elena tried to cover her apprehension with her cheeriest smile.

Señor Cruz proceeded in Spanish, asking Alita what her day would be like tomorrow.

"Mañana tendré un examen de matematicos," she answered, making a sour face. Elena didn't blame her, she hated math tests, too. Then Alita explained that after the test her class would be going to the aquarium. Elena was proud that she understood at least most of what was being said.

Elena noticed that Señor and Señora Cruz spent a lot of time focusing on Alita, giving her space to tell them about her plans the following day. Elena couldn't remember when she'd

ever been handed that much uninterrupted airtime at home.

Jenna joined in the Spanish conversation, stumbling through several questions and answers. Elena wasn't as bold. If she was ever unsure about something, she felt it was best just to stay quiet. Her greatest fear was piping up and having everyone laugh at her. When Señor and Señora Cruz pitched her the occasional question, she answered with nods, shrugs, and the occasional *"sí"* or *"no."*

"Elena, you don't seem to be participating in the Spanish conversation," Señora Cruz observed gently. "Is something wrong?"

Elena thought about it and then answered quietly, *"Estoy embarazada."*

The Cruzes stared at her for a moment and appeared to be doing their best to choke back giggles.

Señora Cruz patted her hand and said in English. "I believe you meant to say you are embarrassed." This is exactly what Elena thought she had said, very clearly. "In *español*, *embarazada* means 'pregnant.' You just told us that you aren't speaking Spanish because you're pregnant."

Elena was the first to laugh out loud. Then Jenna and the Cruzes followed with their own nervous laughter. Although Elena was glad her second flub of the day had happened among nice people, it cemented the idea she'd had earlier that she would rather just listen to people speaking Spanish.

They lingered at dinner, eating slowly while the Cruzes drank more wine. Alita continued to drill Jenna and Elena with questions as night descended over the city and the moon perched outside the living room window, round and white as a china plate. Elena didn't know how long they sat at the dinner table, but it felt like hours. She couldn't remember the last time all six of her own family members sat down together for a meal, much less one that lasted longer than thirty minutes.

After Jenna and Elena helped clear the dinner plates from the table, Señora Cruz gave Jenna blankets and pillows to spread out on the couch.

"That was nice of the Cruzes to put you up," Elena said.

"Oh yeah, I'm totally grateful. They're a nice family." She lowered her voice to a rough whisper. "That little girl, Alita, is a trip. I've never seen someone with so much energy."

"I know. She's a little hyper, but she seems sweet."

"And she certainly isn't shy, which is sort of refreshing. I have two cousins about her age—Bridget's eight and Chloe's ten. I love them, but it takes days just to get them to tell you their favorite color."

Elena smiled and nodded. That's how she remembered herself as a kid.

"What are you taking for your core class?" Elena asked. Each student at the International School was expected to take conversational Spanish, Basque culture, and then choose an elective as their core studies. The students were able to choose from architecture, sculpture, horticulture, or play production.

"Architecture. You?"

"Play production."

"Cool. I thought about that one. It's supposed to be an awesome program. But I'm good at math and I like to draw, so architecture was sort of an obvious choice."

"Makes sense." Elena was a little disappointed that she wouldn't already know someone in her longest class.

"So, what time do you want to head to campus tomorrow?" Jenna asked, switching topics without pause. Elena liked that Jenna just assumed they would walk together. It made her feel as if they were already old friends.

"About eight thirty, I guess. Class doesn't start 'til nine."

"All right." Jenna scooted down under the covers. "I was thinking about going to the beach after class tomorrow. I mean, that's what we're here for, right?"

"Definitely."

"So, I'm thinking we should just wear our bathing suits under our clothes."

"Sounds good to me," Elena said, as she started down the hallway toward the bedroom that she would have all to herself for three months. "Good night."

"Hey, Elena," Jenna called in a singsong voice. "Don't let the Spanish bedbugs bite." She poked her head up over the back of the couch and smiled a crooked, mischievous smile. Elena smiled back and realized how much she wanted to be able to count Jenna among the friends she was planning to make during her time in Spain. She seemed like the kind of girl anyone would want to have in their corner.

Chapter Three

Elena woke to the smell of strong coffee. Once she'd showered and gotten dressed for school, she padded to the kitchen where Señora Cruz offered her a small steaming cup.

"Here, you must try Spanish coffee. You will love it." Elena wasn't usually much of a coffee drinker, but she didn't want to offend Señora Cruz, so she stirred a generous amount of sugar and milk in the cup and took a sip. It was strong, but rich and delicious. Elena could get used to coffee that tasted like this. Jenna joined her at the kitchen table and rubbed at puffy eyes. She ate a sweet roll and sipped her own coffee in silence. Elena guessed she was like Gwen in that it took

her a while to wake up. Elena had learned early on just to give Gwen her space for the first hour of the morning. She decided to do the same thing with Jenna.

After breakfast the two girls packed up their backpacks and headed toward campus in the center of town.

"Why don't we take the promenade," Elena suggested. "It's only a couple of minutes out of our way. We have time."

"Sure."

Elena got a thrill just looking at the beach. She had always wondered what it would be like to live within walking dis- tance of the shore. She pictured herself walking past the beach every morning watching the early sunlight bounce off the water. In her daydream there was a boy by her side, hold- ing her hand and smiling.

"So, do you have a boyfriend back in Phoenix?" Elena ventured after a few minutes of silence.

"No." Jenna laughed. "Not particularly."

"What do you mean?"

"Oh, I was dating a few guys, but nothing serious."

"Oh, right," Elena said, though she had no idea what it felt like to date more than one guy. Actually, she really didn't have much idea what it was like to date one guy. She hadn't had a boyfriend since Robbie Bowers in the seventh grade. And that wasn't all that serious.

"I fall for boys like this." Jenna snapped her fingers. They cut over through the town center and headed away from the ocean. "But then I lose interest just as quick. So I never end up dating any one guy for too long. There are just so many cute boys out there. I don't want to limit myself, you know?"

Elena laughed.

"What's so funny?"

"Oh, it's just that I'm the total opposite. I don't fall in love very often, but when I do, I fall really hard. It's sort of a joke with my sister and some of my friends."

"Do you have someone back home?" Jenna asked.

"I was seeing this guy last year, but that ended badly."

"What happened?"

Normally Elena might have waited longer to share this story with someone she was trying to impress, but Jenna seemed so relaxed and nonjudgmental that she found her-self going into it. "Well, there was this guy I had a huge crush on last year, Joe Cipriani. He was so cute."

Jenna nodded, encouraging her to continue.

"And he just seemed really cool, too. Anyway, somehow he heard that I liked him, and he started flirting with me at school and calling me on my cell. Well, one day he came by my house to study. I left the room to get snacks, and while I was gone he asked my sister out."

"No," Jenna gasped.

Elena nodded solemnly. "He was after her all along."

"What a jerk."

"Yeah."

"But you haven't given up on boys or anything? You still believe in love and all that stuff?"

Elena thought about it for a moment and then answered honestly, "Yeah, I guess I do."

"Well, you're a romantic," Jenna said, bumping Elena's arm playfully with her elbow.

"I guess you could say that."

"We'll have to find you a nice Spanish hottie to fall for."

Elena smiled. "Okay, but I'm definitely going to be more careful this time." Elena wondered if it would really be that easy to change.

They arrived at school with five minutes to find their respective classrooms. With its sleek, smooth walls, high windows edged in steel, and bright red tile rooftops, the campus was jarringly modern compared to the rest of town. The classrooms were laid out in a square with stone-paved pathways zigzagging through a grassy plane. Elena held her class schedule, which had come in a packet of S.A.S.S. material, up next to Jenna's.

"Look, we have conversational Spanish together," Jenna said. "Second period."

"Want to meet at the multimedia center before Spanish?" Elena asked before they parted ways. "We have a fifteen-minute break, and I want to see if I can check my e-mail."

"Sure," Jenna called as she started in the opposite direction across campus. "See you there."

After first period, Elena met Jenna in the multimedia center,

and the two girls snagged available computers and typed in
their student IDs and passwords.

To: dramagirl23@email.com
From: LanieH@email.com
Subject: Hello from Spain!

Hi Claire,

I'm here! Well, my body's here. My mind is still somewhere
else. I guess this is what they call jet lag. That's a good name
for it b/c I'm definitely lagging. I'm still excited to be here. I
can't wait to get started in play production and start connecting with the Spaniard in me—I know it has just been hiber-
nating all these years. It really is a culture shock here,
though. It's hard to explain. Imagine walking down the street
without recognizing anyone, not knowing which streets lead
where, and not speaking the language. I wish you were with
me so we could figure this place out together!

The good news is that my host family is really cool. The
mother weighs about 10 pounds, and the dad is quite the
fashion plate. They have a daughter named Alita. She's a
riot. She loves anything American. I'm unique and interesting
just because I'm from the States. That was easy! I also had
a surprise housemate. There was a flood in the dorms, so a
girl named Jenna is staying with my family for a few nights.

She's really outgoing and unflappable, so I think she'll be a good person for me to hang out with here. I miss you mucho!

Love,

Elena in Spain-a

Elena and Jenna logged off and scurried to their Spanish class, taking their seats just before the bell rang. Their Spanish teacher, Señor Gonzalez, handed out worksheets and began giving the class a first-day rundown similar to the one Elena had just sat through in Basque culture. Elena guessed that Señor Gonzalez was older than the mountains that towered over Playa de la Concha. He spoke in clipped tones and spent an inordinate amount of time going over the multitude of rules for his class. He even looked tough and weathered, with steel wool curls and a grave face. Elena could tell there wouldn't be a lot of goofing around in Señor Gonzalez's class.

"I want you to speak Spanish at all times in this class. I may occasionally ask questions in English, but I expect you to answer me in Spanish. Of course, that doesn't mean you should expect to be fluent right away. I just want you to try."

"How do we know when we've become fluent?" a guy named Dwight asked, as if grasping a language was something you could quantify and measure.

"There isn't a line you cross and suddenly you're fluent in a language," Señor Gonzales explained. Dwight's face fell. "However," Señor Gonzales continued, his finger punching through the air in front of him. "Many people say that you can be considered fluent once you dream in Spanish. It is then that the language and the culture become so much a part of you that they find their way into your subconscious."

Elena promised herself that by the time she left San Sebastián, she would be dreaming in Spanish.

Elena spotted a familiar face as soon as she'd entered her last class of the day, play production. Alex made eye contact with her on her way in and patted the empty seat beside him. With Jenna in her Spanish class and now Alex in play production, she was feeling like quite the social butterfly.

"A play is not just a bunch of words on paper. It's an entire world created by a playwright and then brought to life," their teacher, Ms. Bartholomew, declared. "This term you will not only learn how to create your own world and bring it to life, but you will also learn how to come together as an artistic community." As she said this, she interlaced the fingers of both hands and stood for a moment for maximum impact. Elena glanced at the faces of the other students. She saw some eyes rolling, heard some whispers and giggles, but mostly there were blank expressions. They were only minutes into the class and Alex was already dozing, with his chin propped on his fist and his black baseball hat pulled down low over his eyes so that at a glance it looked as though he was concentrating on his notes.

Ms. Bartholomew, or Ms. B, as she had asked to be

called, seemed to be a different breed of teacher than the ones Elena had been introduced to earlier in the day. For one thing, she ditched the stodgy polyester pants, button-front shirts, and bland sweater sets. Ms. B wore shell jewelry around her neck and wrists, and a flowing white linen dress cinched with a turquoise-studded leather belt. She wasn't one of those unkempt, I'm-pretending-it's-still-the-sixties hippies. She was a sleeker, more modern version.

Although Elena could tell from their expressions that some of the students already thought Ms. B had just stepped off the mother ship, Elena warmed to her. At least she cared about what she was teaching. Elena had plenty of teachers at home who showed up every day and seemed to sleepwalk through class, regurgitating the same lectures they'd been giving for twenty-five years without even bothering to update the pop-culture references in their halfhearted jokes. Only last year her history teacher referred to Will Smith as the Fresh Prince. Talk about out of touch.

"The main determinant of your grade in this class will be the final project, a full-length play! If you're lucky enough to be the cream of the crop, you'll stage your play and perform it at the end of the term." Ms. B clapped her hands and smiled broadly, as though no sane person could possibly wish for anything more. "We are only going to be able to stage two plays—the top two, as judged by me. However, even if your play isn't chosen for the final performance, you will still be involved in some way. We'll need people to design

costumes and props. You might be acting in a role or helping to design the sets or lighting. In a couple of weeks you'll
form groups of two and three...." Some of the students,
including Elena, groaned after this last remark. She hated
group projects. Somehow she always got stuck with some
bossy know-it-all who took over the whole project and
wouldn't listen to anyone else's ideas. Though she was
dreading the idea of a group project, she was also already
picturing herself as one of the winners. In her mind, she was
standing just offstage, watching as the stars of her play
received a standing ovation. As the crowd roared, the actors
grabbed her by the hand and insisted she come onstage and
take a bow with them.

"Now class." Ms. B clapped her hands together again
fiercely, breaking Elena's daydream. Alex woke with a snort,
and his chin slipped off his hand. He teetered in his chair but
was able to regain his composure without spilling onto the
floor. Elena covered her mouth to smother a giggle.

Alex straightened in his chair and pushed the bill of his
hat farther up on his forehead. Elena had decided this was
his subconscious way of letting the world know he was once
again part of the living.

Two hours later the bell rang, signaling the end of the school
day. Kids scrambled to jam their notebooks into their backpacks and rush out the door.

"So, you're going to the beach after this, too, huh?" Alex

said, glancing at the thin strap of Elena's bikini top peeking out of the neckline of her T-shirt. She'd followed Jenna's advice and donned the suit under her clothes, and a beach towel stuffed in her backpack.

"Yeah. Are you going surfing?" she asked as she followed him through the classroom door and out into the midday sunshine.

He nodded languidly and picked up a short board that was propped against the wall outside. "I already went once this morning, but it's not like I have any homework to do on the first day of school."

As they walked together toward the beach, they passed a cluster of tall, aging buildings huddled together under a towering hill that formed the *parte vieja*, the oldest and most historical part of town.

"Have you been in there yet?" Alex pointed toward the alleyways that cut through the buildings like caverns.

"No. Have you?"

"Yeah. It's awesome. It feels like a time warp. Come walk through for a minute," he said, leading her between two grayish-brown buildings so close together it looked as though they were closing in on each other. The air cooled as soon as she stepped onto the rutted street. The proximity of the buildings blocked much of the sun, so it felt like a perpetually cloudy day. Some of the walls were marred by spray-painted graffiti written in Basque. Alex led her through the maze of narrow streets.

"It looks like there's a bar or restaurant on every corner," Elena said.

"Yeah. I've heard this is where everyone comes to eat and party. Hey, want to get something to eat now?"

Elena looked at her watch. She was late meeting Jenna. "I should get going. I'm meeting a friend at the beach."

"All right," he said as he walked toward a tapas bar with an ABIERTO sign in the window. "Maybe I'll see you out there."

Elena headed back into the sunlight and started toward the ocean. Once she reached the beach she slipped off her flip-flops and stepped onto the simmering sand. After scanning the packs of sunbathers, she finally caught a glimpse of Jenna's blond hair shining in the afternoon glare. She was wearing a red bikini with a thin bandeau top and skinny bottoms tied in little bows at the sides. The strips of fabric looked as if they might fall off if she rolled over too quickly or breathed wrong. On either side of Jenna's towel was a girl lounging on her own towel.

"Hey, there," Elena said once she had strolled over to the girls. She did a little hot-sand dance in place as she spread her towel out next to the voluptuous girl to Jenna's right. Elena wiggled out of her tank top and shorts and lay down.

"What's up, Elena?" Jenna lifted herself up on her elbows and peered at her over the top of her oversized movie star sunglasses. "This is Caitlin and Marci. They're from the same high school in Boston. We're in Basque culture together."

Elena gave them both a little wave. Simply judging them by their looks, Marci and Caitlin appeared to be polar opposites. Marci was small and skinny with straight black bobbed hair that skimmed her chin. Caitlin was tall and buxom with a wide, toothy smile and loose ringlets—all curves and curls.

"We were just debating the whole topless thing," Jenna said, nodding discreetly toward a cluster of Spanish women lying out in only their tiny bikini bottoms, and then toward another group of women reading French *Vogue* and looking just as bare, their brown skin almost entirely exposed to the sun and everything else.

"Oh," Elena gasped, genuinely surprised. She immediately regretted sounding like such a prude. She looked around and sure enough, a little less than half the women on the beach were sans tops. For some reason she hadn't noticed until now. She'd been too lost in the beauty of the ocean and the sky—swimming in her own little world of thought, as usual.

"So, would you?" Jenna asked. The girls stared at her, leaning in for her answer.

"Would I what?"

"Go topless."

"Uh, well. I'm not sure," Elena stammered, not knowing if she meant now or sometime in the very distant future. She didn't want to be the party pooper, but she was seriously doubtful about taking her top off in public. It took a lot just to get out here in her bikini. "What do you guys think?" she asked, lobbing the question to the two girls she'd just met.

"I don't think anyone would even notice if I went topless," Marci said, looking down at the two triangles of material barely poking out from her chest.

"What about you, Caitlin?" Jenna seemed to be getting into this, counting Marci's ambivalence as a vote in favor of yanking the tops.

"No way," she said, shaking her head violently. "These babies stay right where they are."

Elena didn't blame her. Caitlin seemed to be getting enough unwanted stares as it was.

"Come on, you guys. We're in a foreign country. When in Rome, you're supposed to do as the Romans do, or whatever that phrase is."

Elena looked away, pretending to watch a little boy splashing in the waves. Caitlin just shook her head.

"All right, let's do it, Marci. It's not like we're going to see anyone we know," Jenna said, sitting up and fiddling with the clasp of her top. Marci shrugged and began pulling at the string tied behind her neck.

"Hey, Elena, what's up?" Elena looked up to see Alex ambling toward the girls, a surfboard tucked under his arm. Marci gasped, and her hands flew up to her chest just in time to catch the triangles of fabric before they flopped down onto her stomach. Jenna casually refastened the clasp of her top. If she was rattled at all, she didn't show it.

Alex set his board down on the sand in front of the girls' feet and sat cross-legged on top of it. Jenna immediately switched into flirt mode, pulling her knees up and sliding her big Jackie-O sunglasses down the bridge of her nose. Alex was mesmerized.

Elena decided to let them flirt in peace. She flipped over onto her stomach and watched a pair of mothers herd their suntanned children toward the showers. The kids had beautiful lithe limbs and delicate features. Elena took in their smooth, dark skin and wondered if she had possibly been switched at birth. Her brothers and sister had inherited their mom's Spanish skin—the color of coffee with lots of cream—and her dark, shiny hair. Although Elena was the only one named after a Spanish relative, she didn't look Spanish. She glanced down at her white arms, which were already turning a mottled pink color from the intense sun. As she reached for the sunscreen tucked in her bag, she heard Alex saying something about the tapas bars in the *parte vieja*.

"So, what do you think?" he asked the group. "Don't you think it'd be cool if we could get some friends together to check out the tapas bars this weekend?"

"I'm in," Jenna agreed quickly.

Marci and Caitlin echoed Jenna's response, and Elena said it sounded like fun.

"Cool. Let's meet Friday night at, like, nine. I'll talk to you about it at school this week."

"If you know any other guys, you should bring them

52

along on Friday." Marci tossed the idea out casually.

"All right." Alex began to stand. "I have to take off. I'll see you in class tomorrow, Elena."

"Okay," she said as she squirted a blob of sunscreen onto her palm and began smearing it on her arms. "If you're early, save me a seat."

He nodded and then said good-bye to the rest of the girls, though his gaze seemed to linger a little longer on Jenna. While Caitlin and Marci returned his good-bye, Jenna just smiled slyly and tipped her head back in a good-bye nod. Alex flashed one more wide smile and strolled away.

"He was nice," Caitlin said once Alex was out of earshot.

"He certainly thought you were nice," Marci teased, poking Jenna in the ribs.

Jenna shrugged. "He was all right."

"What do you mean, he was all right? You were all over him," Elena cried. From the way Jenna had transformed so quickly into Marilyn Monroe, Elena had assumed she'd found the love of her life.

"I know. I'm so bad. I just like to flirt." Jenna laughed.

"Well, you're very good at it," Elena returned, laughing now as well.

Jenna struck a fashion pose on her towel. "Thank you, dahling," she drawled like an old-time movie star, throwing her head back dramatically.

After a couple of hours at the beach Elena decided to leave. There would be plenty of time to get a tan, she rea-

soned. The last thing she wanted to do on her first full day in San Sebastián was to stay at the beach too long and end up glowing like a boiled lobster. When she stood up to put her clothes on and stuff her towel and sunscreen back into her bulging backpack, Jenna stood, too.

"I'll go with you," she said, slipping on a pair of shorts.

They left Marci and Caitlin, and trudged through the soft sand and up the stairs that led to the promenade. Elena stopped for a moment at the top to take it all in, the sea, the sunbathers, the tiny boats bobbing at the horizon. She tried to take in the scenery the way a filmmaker would, as a shot on a wide-screen lens. If she were scripting this moment, she'd linger on a shot of the sea and then write, "Fade out."

As the girls headed up the hill toward the Cruzes' apartment, Jenna veered off their path for a moment and strolled over to a shawl of bougainvillea that dripped down the wall of an apartment building from a balcony above. Jenna plucked a sprig of magenta flowers from the dangling vine and tucked it behind her ear. Then she twisted off another piece and helped Elena wind it through her thick ponytail.

"You look hot," Jenna exclaimed as she stepped back to take in the sight of Elena, who smiled shyly and felt a little goofy standing on the sidewalk dripping in petals. "We needed a little color." The girls fell back into step. Elena felt the eyes of some passersby brushing over them. She wasn't used to drawing attention to herself. Her instinct was to shrink away from it. But Jenna, strutting unself-consciously beside her in a bikini top and a crown of pink flowers, had a way of making things seem less goofy.

When they arrived at the Cruz apartment, Alita bounded to the door to greet them.

"Did you go to the beach today?" She followed them through the foyer and into the living room.

"We did," Elena answered.

"I am not allowed to go during the week, only weekends," she explained, then turned her attention back to Jenna. "Maybe you can take me with you this weekend."

"Sure, maybe," Jenna answered.

"What are you doing now? Do you want to go for a walk?"

"Well, we were outside all afternoon," Elena offered as gently as possible.

"Why don't you read magazines with us in Elena's room," Jenna suggested.

"Yes. American magazines," Alita sang as she motored down the hall and into Elena's room before the older girls even had time to set their backpacks down by the door.

Señor Cruz walked through the front door at half-past eight, and Señora Cruz called them all to dinner twenty minutes later. The three girls put down their magazines and joined Señor and Señora Cruz and Alita at the round dinner table. Elena gathered that the Cruzes' normal dinnertime was close to nine o'clock in the evening. She made a mental note to check with another student who lived with a host family

in town to see if it was a Spanish thing or a Cruz thing.

After a leisurely dinner of paella, Elena and Jenna cleared the dishes and offered to wash up. Elena had been so travel-weary the night before that she hadn't even thought to offer her help. She knew her mother would be mortified.

Elena stood at the sink scrubbing the pans and plates, while Jenna sopped them with a dish towel and then lined them up in the drying rack.

"Do you wash the dishes at home?" Alita asked from the table where Señora Cruz was helping her with her home-work.

"Uh-huh. We all have chores, and mine is to do the din-ner dishes," Elena explained.

"How many people do you clean up after, Elena?"

"Six when my brother Jeremy is home from college."

"That is a big job," Señora Cruz nodded to show her approval of Elena's work ethic. Elena didn't tell her that at home all she had to do was squirt the dishes with water, stack them in the dishwasher, and flip a switch. "And what about you, Jenna?"

"We have a housekeeper," Jenna murmured.

"I have chores," Alita interrupted. "I clean my room and sweep the balcony, and I help Mama with the groceries."

"Sí, estás muy útil," Señora cooed. "She is...is it an American phrase...my little helper?"

"Yes, that's a phrase. She's your little helper." Elena smiled over at Alita, who lit up. Señora Cruz kissed Alita, and then scooted her off to bed. Elena could hear her stop to kiss her father good night in the living room.

Elena rinsed the last dish in her pile and handed it to Jenna. She pulled the stopper in the sink and watched the murky water slide down the drain and putter out at the end.

"That was the last one," Jenna announced to Señora Cruz.

"Thank you so much for helping, girls." Señora Cruz took the wet dish towel from Jenna and hung it on a rack in the corner to dry. "You are good workers."

"Thank you for dinner," Elena said.

"The meal was wonderful," Jenna piped in, as Señora Cruz left the room.

"You can use the bathroom first," Elena offered to Jenna.

After Jenna padded toward the back of the apartment a hush settled over the small kitchen. There were only a few sounds in the apartment. The ancient window that stood over the sink was shoved open, allowing a cool night breeze to waft in. Elena could hear a car's tires crunching on the nearly empty gravel road outside, and music playing in one of the apartments across the alley. She couldn't recall a time in her own house when things were still long enough for her to pause and consider each soft, distinct sound.

Chapter Four

On Thursday, Elena broke her routine of hanging out in the sun-drenched quad during the break before play production. Instead, she'd rushed to the multimedia center as soon as the bell rang in order to snag an empty computer and check her e-mail.

To: LanieH@email.com
From: gwenrunner@email.com
Subject: Miss you!!!

Spain or Shine

Hi Lanie,

How are you, Señorita? (See, I can speak Spanish, too.) I still can't believe you actually did it—you went to Spain by yourself. What do you think of it so far? Have you made any friends yet? Are the Spanish boys cute?

School starts next Tuesday, after Labor Day. I'm already busy with track, and the occasional party. Caleb is practicing with his little garage band and playing football, and Jeremy leaves for UCLA in a few weeks. I can tell he's antsy to get back to school. UCLA starts so late and most of his friends from home have already left.

I miss you so much already. We all do. Our bedroom feels so empty. It makes me sad for the time when I go away to college. But that's still a year away. Write soon... I'm bored here in boringville.

Love,

Gwennie

p.s. Mom says remember to call Great-Aunt Elena to set a date to visit her and the cousins.

p.p.s. She just came in the room and made me write that.

To: gwenrunner@email.com
From: LanieH@email.com
Subject: Re: Miss you!!!

San Sebastián is gorgeous. I'm so happy to be here. I have to say I don't feel any more Spanish yet, but hopefully that will change by the time I leave here tanned and fluent.

I have met some cool people though. One of my new friends, Jenna, is rooming with me and my host family for a while because of some problems with her dorm room. She's funny and outgoing and the total opposite of me.

No, I haven't met any cute Spanish boys yet. I have met one guy so far—Alex. He is cute but he's not Spanish and he's definitely not my type. He reminds me a little of Caleb actually, a mix of adventure and laid-back attitude, which is a great thing to find in a friend or a brother, don't you think? Miss you tons.

Love,

Elena

Elena logged off and made her way to the quad to see if she might catch Alex on his way to class and walk with him. She spotted him near the fountain talking to Jenna.

"Hi, you guys," she called as she ambled over to her friends. "What's going on?"

"Elena, we were just talking about you." Alex tipped his head back in order to peer out from beneath the bill of his hat. "Are you still up for going to the tapas bars tomorrow night?"

"Sure. I'm in if you guys are."

Alex nodded enthusiastically. "Totally."

"I'll talk to Marci and Caitlin about it in Basque culture next period and make sure they're still planning on meeting up, too," Jenna said.

"Cool. Let's meet at nine at the Plaza de la Constitución," Alex suggested. "It's in the middle of the old part of town."

Jenna agreed to tell Marci and Caitlin about their arrangements and then sprinted to her Basque culture class. Elena hustled toward Ms. B's class, prodding Alex to hurry up.

"Alex, I know you can walk faster than that. We're going to be late again." After only a few days of walking to class with Alex, Elena had already noticed that both of them had a tendency to regard time as a relative thing. Elena didn't even own a watch, but she had resolved not to be as flaky here as she had been at home. Last year she was late so often to algebra that her teacher had threatened to take points off her final if she wasn't sitting in her seat before the bell rang.

Elena and Alex slid into class just as the bell marking the beginning of the period rang. Ms. B began chirping about the role of conflict in a play. Alex scratched a note at the bottom of his notebook, tapped Elena's shoe with the toe of his own, and shoved the notebook out to the edge of his desk so she could steal a glimpse.

What's Jenna's situation? Does she have a guy back home?

She was surprised Alex was taking any initiative. For the past few days he seemed to be just having a little fun flirting,

like Jenna. Elena slid a sheet of paper out of her own notebook and responded

I think she's available. Are you going to make a move?

Alex wrote:

Not sure…maybe.

"Okay, does anyone have questions about conflict?" Ms. B
asked, panning the room. Elena liked that Ms. B always
allowed the shy students, like herself, enough time to work up
the courage to raise their hands. "Good. Now then, your first
assignment will be to apply conflict in a dramatic situation." Ms.
B wrote FIRST WRITING ASSIGNMENT DUE TUESDAY on the
whiteboard in large black letters. "I want you to think about a
conflict you have experienced recently and dramatize it. It
could be an argument with someone, a debate, or even a problem accomplishing something."

Out of the corner of her eye, Elena saw a thin arm shoot
up into the air. It was a familiar sight by now. The arm
belonged to Dylan, the only girl with a pierced lip Elena had
ever met. Her hair was black as ink, and she wore smudgy
kohl eye shadow around her almond-shaped eyes. On Elena
that eye makeup would look trashy, but on Dylan it looked
model-cool. Dylan was attentive in class and seemed serious
about playwriting. Elena knew right away that she was going
to have the best work in class. "Yes, Dylan?" Ms. B nodded
in her direction.

"Ms. B, can we use a fictional conflict?"

"I'm going to say no this time, Dylan. I admire your ambition, but we'll get to fiction later in the semester. This is just to get an idea of conflict. Anything else?"

Elena glanced at Dylan. She couldn't decide how she felt about this girl. On the one hand, she was impressed by her knowledge and ambition. But she also felt a stab of jealousy. Dylan was obviously going to be her toughest competition.

Elena was kneeling on the floor of her room watching Jenna pull shirts from a bottomless black suitcase. It was Friday night, and Jenna was trying to figure out what to wear to the tapas bars. She had dragged her suitcase into Elena's tiny room so they could try on outfits together in front of the full-length mirror Señora Cruz had propped against one wall. Elena had decided on jeans and a pink top twenty minutes earlier. She offered her advice as Jenna pulled tops on, and then yanked them off moments later, flinging them on the floor as she vetoed each one.

"I'm almost ready—I swear," Jenna called as she buzzed around the room in a skirt and bra, limping on one wedge sandal and searching for the other. "What do you think?" Jenna asked, holding up a trendy green top.

"Cute," Elena said.

"Hmm," Jenna turned and considered herself in the mirror. "No, it makes me look fat."

"Oh, please," Elena groaned. Jenna took off the shirt, revealing a perfectly flat belly.

Jenna finally decided on the first shirt she'd tried on—a

plain white tank top—with dangly earrings. Elena waited another ten minutes as Jenna combed through the mess on the floor in search of her purse. She finally found it shoved beneath Elena's bed. The girls hastily piled the clothes back in Jenna's suitcase, then said good-bye to the Cruzes.

"Have a good time," Señora Cruz called. "Please be back by twelve." Elena's curfew at home was eleven thirty. She'd always held the suspicion that those extra thirty minutes could mean the difference between a fair evening and a truly memorable night. She was ready to find out.

The sun was sinking into the ocean as Elena and Jenna veered from the promenade toward the dorms. They hooked up with Marci and Caitlin at the front entrance of the dorm building as planned, and then headed out as a group toward the tapas bars to meet Alex.

As they entered the alleyways, the streetlights above the doorways were already lit and glowing fuzzy yellow. Alex was waiting at the Plaza de la Constitución with a blond guy.

"Hey," Alex called as the four girls approached. "This is Chris. Chris, this is Elena, Jenna, Marci, and Caitlin."

Chris offered each girl a polite handshake. Elena marveled at how much he looked like Alex. They could have been brothers. Chris wore baggy pants, a long-sleeve Billabong shirt, and a knit cap pulled down low over salt-ravaged hair. He was an all-American, California surfer boy in every way. That was why Elena practically lost her balance when he said, "Pleasure meeting you," in a distinctly British accent.

"Wait. You're English?" Elena blurted before she could stop herself.

"Yes." He nodded, clearly surprised by her reaction.

"Right. Of course." She snapped her jaw shut and pumped his hand. "Well, it's nice to meet you."

"Hey, Jenna," Alex said casually.

"What's up?" She tossed him a sweet little smile. Elena thought she saw them hold each other's gaze for a couple extra moments before Alex cut the silence.

"So, where should we go first?" Alex asked. They stood together watching the other diners strolling through the cobbled streets beside them, ambling in and out of open doorways and flocking around bars. The plan was to hop from bar to bar, tasting tapas at each place.

"Okay, I have a plan," Jenna announced. "It's easy to find out where the best place is. You just have to figure out where the locals are going."

"But they're going all over the place," Caitlin interjected.

Jenna scanned the crowd, ignoring Caitlin's comment. "There," she shouted, then lowering her voice. "Follow those two." She pointed in the direction of a chic Spanish couple in matching tight Versace pants.

They tailed the young Spanish couple to a bright and airy bar. Bullfighting posters lined the walls, and cured hams hung from the ceilings. But the focal point of the restaurant was clearly the bar. Flocks of patrons stood chatting and drinking and nibbling from a collection of plates, each one

nesting a small portion of food. Elena and her friends found an open spot where the bar curved toward the wall. They squeezed in and waited.

"Why isn't anyone taking our order?" Caitlin groaned. It did seem that everyone around them was munching happily, while they were being ignored.

"I wonder if there's an age limit," Elena ventured.

"Definitely not," Jenna returned. "They would have carded us on the way in. Maybe we have to wave someone down."

"First time at a tapas bar, eh?" inquired the cute young guy standing beside Elena at the bar. They looked over at a boy with shaggy hair and rumpled clothes who spoke with what sounded like an Australian accent. "You just grab what you want and tell the bartender later."

"How does he know you ate what you said you did?" Jenna asked.

"He doesn't. It's the honor system," he returned. "Are you honorable?" This last question was playfully directed at Jenna.

"Who me?" Jenna asked with mock innocence. "Of course."

Caitlin rolled her eyes and cut in. "So, we just grab these things and start eating?" she asked, leaning in for a plate of skewered shrimp.

Elena glanced at Alex to gauge his reaction to Jenna's newest flirtation, but he had already struck up a conversation with the Spanish couple they'd followed to the bar.

"What'll you ladies have to drink?" their new friend asked.

"I'll just have a Coke," Elena responded as she reached for a plate of stuffed mushrooms.

"A Coke?" Jenna shook her head. "There's only one thing to drink at tapas bars. Sangrias all around."

Elena shrugged and popped a mushroom into her mouth, then switched places with Jenna at the bar so she could be closer to the boy of the moment. They learned his name was Paul, and he was actually from New Zealand. "I'm traveling for a while before I head back home and start working for my mum and dad," he explained.

"How long is a while?" Jenna asked.

"I'm not sure. Until my money runs out, I guess."

While Jenna flirted with Paul, Elena stood with Marci, Caitlin, and the boys—all of them sliding plates back and forth around the bar like a game of checkers. They started cautiously with dishes that looked familiar and unthreatening, sautéed mushrooms and bacon, cheeses, olives, and *pan con tomate*—bread with tomatoes.

The female half of the Spanish couple they'd followed to the bar introduced herself to everyone as Arrosa. She was friendly even though no one in the group spoke Spanish particularly well.

"Usted debe tratar éstos," she said, pointing to what looked like it might be stuffed squid. Elena kept quiet, but she was surprised how well Alex and Chris were able to communicate with the Spanish couple. With Arrosa's guid-

ance, the whole group soon began to venture into the unknown, popping morsels into their mouths that they didn't recognize and couldn't pronounce.

"You should try the ham, too," a woman with a French accent leaned over to say. "It's their specialty." Elena hoped they wouldn't pull one of the hams from the ceiling and slice it up in front of her.

She tried a timid bite of some ham from a plate in front of her. "Oh, that's really good. Thanks for the suggestion."

Most of the people at the bar had a dish to recommend or a story to tell. Elena was beginning to realize that the whole tapas bar experience was as much about the company as it was about the food.

"I think I'm ready to move on," Jenna said, after they'd been at the bar for about an hour.

"How come? Aren't you having fun?" Elena asked, raising her voice to compete with the growing chorus of voices around them.

"Yeah, but the whole point is to hit several different places. We have to be home by midnight, right? So I think it's time to move on." Jenna took another sip of her purpley-red sangria. Elena had a similar glass with hunks of fruit bobbing in it, though she'd hardly had any of it. It was too sweet, and the smell of wine and cinnamon made her dizzy, so she just took small sips now and then to seem agreeable.

"That Spanish couple at the bar told me of a cool place to go, a locals' place," Marci suggested, barely concealing the pride she took in one-upping Jenna in the competition to find the coolest place in town.

Alex and Chris squeezed through the cramped bar, while Elena and the other girls grabbed hands to form a human chain so that they wouldn't get separated. They all spilled out into the street in front of the restaurant.

Marci led them past several discos where Trikitixas— Basque pop music—came thundering out into the street whenever the doors opened. They wandered out toward the cathedral at the edge of the old section of town, and stopped in front of a restaurant that had a Basque sign mounted above the door by rusty nails.

"This is it; I'm sure of it," Marci said. She opened the door to an inviting, lively place. The lighting was soft and rosy, and flamenco guitar played live in the back of the restaurant. They walked up to the bar, and Elena took her time looking over the array of choices. Finally she leaned into the bar and stretched out to grasp the rim of a plate of prosciutto rolls— melon and figs wrapped in thin cured ham. She pulled the plate toward her and felt a tap on her shoulder.

As she started to turn, her eyes fell on the profile of a Spanish boy several paces down the bar. She couldn't help but pause midmotion. It was like stumbling upon a treasure at a yard sale—a beautiful surprise. He was taller and more muscular than most of the Spanish boys she'd seen and his face was leading-man perfect. For a moment the only sound she could hear was her own heart thumping inside her

69

chest. Then he turned and looked right at her. She glanced away quickly as a rush of blood filled her cheeks.

She felt the tap on her shoulder again and turned to answer Jenna. When Elena looked up again, the boy was gone. It seemed no one else had spotted him. Even Jenna, with her finely tuned boy radar, had missed him.

As the night progressed, she caught glimpses of him. He stuck near a knot of local guys, his comrades for the evening. She noticed several girls squeeze their way into the cluster of boys, hanging conspicuously close to the cute one.

Jenna marched out onto the little dance floor in the center of the room. Within seconds, a boy with thick shiny curls was showing her some flamenco dance moves. Although Jenna's feet and hands flopped awkwardly, she didn't seem to care. She just twirled and pranced around the dance floor, letting out one of her wide, head-thrown-back laughs.

After a while Jenna took a break and wandered over to Elena and Marci at the bar. As Jenna and Marci talked about the boy with the curls, Elena imagined how much easier life would be as Jenna. She pictured how she would be if she were as confident as Jenna. That version of herself would walk right up to the Spanish guy and introduce herself. She'd slink close enough to brush his arm with hers, but she wouldn't hover. He would tell her his name and ask her a question, and then she'd make one of the flirtatious jokes Jenna was always making.

"Hola," a low voice cut through the air around her, the

weight of it pulling her back down to earth. Elena turned to find the very boy she'd been envisioning standing beside her, close enough to touch. She hadn't even noticed him approaching her. He was saying something.

"Oh, hi," she managed to squeak before he had to repeat his greeting again.

"I'm Miguel," he said in clear English.

"Elena," she said, though her voice came from someplace outside herself. Her name sounded strange. She didn't feel like herself.

"Elena. That's a Spanish name, no? Are you Spanish?"

"Um no, well yeah, sort of." This had to be the worst conversation in history. She wondered why he was even talking to her. She stared at the collar of his shirt to avoid meeting his eyes. "Actually, my mom is Spanish. I mean she's American, but she has Spanish heritage. So I'm part Spanish." She'd recovered, sort of.

He looked as if he was about to ask her another question when Jenna joined the conversation.

"Hey," she said, grabbing Elena's arm but beaming at Miguel.

"Hello." He nodded politely. "This is your friend?" he asked, turning toward Elena.

"Oh, sorry. Yes. This is Jenna." Jenna's hand was already stretched out to meet his.

"What's your name?" Jenna asked, tilting her head to one side.

"Miguel. Nice to meet you." His eyes were stuck to Jenna. Elena could feel herself disappearing.

"Miguel, that's a nice name. Are you a local?" Jenna asked, leaning in toward him and looking interested.

"Yes. I live in the part of town called Gros. It is on the other side of the river. Where are you ladies from?"

"Oh, we're *ladies,* are we?"

Miguel chuckled softly and looked down where he scuffed the floor with his shoe. Elena just stood there as Jenna carried on a conversation with this boy named Miguel that sounded much like the one Elena had scripted in her head. It seemed as easy as breathing for Jenna. Miguel was chuckling now at something Jenna had said. Suddenly, his interest in Elena became clear. He had obviously approached Elena as a way of getting close to Jenna, who had been standing just beside her. She was ashamed she hadn't seen this coming, particularly after the situation with Joe Cipriani. How could she have fallen for that move twice?

"Well, it was a pleasure meeting you both," he said finally. "Perhaps I will see you again."

"I hope so," Jenna cooed. Elena managed a smile.

He started to walk back over to his friends. Before he had even reached the group he was intercepted by a girl in a low-cut halter who clung to his arm. Someone who received that much unsolicited attention from girls had to be full of himself. Elena decided she was better off where she had begun and where she had ended, at a distance.

Chapter Five

In all of Elena's daydreams about San Sebastián during the months leading up to her semester abroad, not once was it raining. In her mind it was a place impervious to rain. Yet, on Saturday morning the gentle tapping on the tile roof of the Cruzes' apartment sounded completely natural. A little rain made sense in San Sebastián. How else could the mountains stay so green and the flowers so full of color?

"What do you think of Alex?" Elena asked from her bed, where she was watching Jenna paint her toenails. The two girls were rehashing the previous night's festivities.

"He's cute. I think he's into Marci, though."

"Are you crazy? He's into you. He was asking me about you the other day in class."

"Oh? What did he say?" Jenna didn't look up. Elena could tell she was trying to play it cool.

"He asked me if you had a boyfriend back home."

"What'd you tell him?" Jenna asked.

"I said you were available." Elena smirked. "He likes you. I think you guys would be so perfect together."

"You do? Well, I've only been in San Sebastián for a week—there are still so many boys I have to meet."

Elena rolled onto her back and stared up at the ceiling. "Like that guy Miguel we met at the end of the night?" Even though Elena had promised herself she would keep a distance from him, she was curious if Jenna liked him since he was so obviously into her.

"He was pretty cute." Jenna shrugged.

Pretty cute, Elena thought. *He was gorgeous.* Before Elena could respond, Señora Cruz opened the door a crack and poked her head through.

"Jenna, you have a phone call from the dormitory manager."

After speaking with the dorm manager, Jenna announced that her room was clean and dry and ready for her to move back in.

"The manager wants me in by this afternoon," Jenna explained.

"You're leaving?" Alita whimpered. "Will you still come to visit?"

"Of course," Jenna assured her, giving Alita a hug.

Alita hovered close to Jenna as she gathered her cosmetics from the bathroom and stowed her stray clothes in empty pockets of her duffel bag. Elena helped fold some of the shirts Jenna had left scattered across the floor after her mini-fashion show the previous night.

Señora Cruz offered to give Jenna a ride. Alita tagged along, but Elena preferred to say good-bye at the house.

"Want to go to the beach tomorrow if it's not raining?" Jenna asked as she headed out the door.

"Sure," Elena returned. She didn't want to make it seem like a big deal, but she was relieved that Jenna didn't equate leaving the Cruz household with leaving Elena behind for good as well.

"See ya tomorrow," Jenna called as she disappeared down the stairway. Elena could hear Jenna's sandals clicking on the stairs, followed by the clunk of her duffel as it hit each step on her way down to the street.

Elena shut the front door and walked into the quiet kitchen. Señor Cruz was sitting at the kitchen table huddled over a cup of steaming coffee and reading *El País*, Spain's national newspaper. He looked up as she entered.

"*Hola,* Elena. *Café?*" he offered, nodding toward the nearly full French press on the stove.

"Oh, no, thanks. I think I'm going to do some homework."

"Good idea," he answered, turning back toward the window next to him, where drops of water ran down the glass. "I have always thought rainy days were good for working."

Elena smiled. "Me, too." She liked that Señor Cruz didn't have to start up a long conversation every time they were alone together. It reminded her of being with her own dad— a quiet comfort.

Elena went to her room, slipped on her iPod headphones, and cued up some old Nick Drake. It was great for studying. She glanced at the slick cover of her Spanish textbook. Her first Spanish term paper was due Tuesday, and she hadn't even begun to think about it. She sat on the bed and pulled the textbook onto her lap. Her pen was poised above a crisp blank sheet of paper, but she couldn't focus on the Spanish assignment. Instead she found her mind wandering through possibilities for the first playwriting assignment, which was also due on Tuesday. She was itching to get started. She shoved the textbook aside and began sketching out a scene.

Last spring she and Gwen had gotten into an argument over who should be able to wear the Tracy Reese dress they shared. With both of their money put together they had been able to afford the dress, but sharing caused some conflicts. Well, actually only one. Elena put her pen to paper and started scribbling.

Their fight over the dress had come the day after Joe Cipriani had asked Gwen out. That was when she had convinced herself Gwen would always end up with the things Elena wanted. She worked a couple lines of dialogue into the beginning to make it clear that this argument was about more than just sharing a dress.

As she wrote she was unaware of anything going on around her. She didn't hear Alita and Señora Cruz come home. She didn't notice when the rain stopped. The only things that existed in the world were the scene, her pen, and the sheet of paper where her thoughts unfolded.

When she was done, she set her pen down and glanced up at the clock. She was stunned to find that two hours had passed. She'd been so absorbed she hadn't even noticed.

Elena peeped out the window and was surprised to find a slice of yellow sunlight showing through a break in the clouds. She was giddy about the scene she'd written, and there was one person she wished she could share it with. She missed Claire. She knew one of the reasons she'd come to Spain was to meet new people, but at that moment she longed for the easy comfort of an old friend.

Elena walked into the front room and called out to Señora Cruz, who was cleaning up in the kitchen.

"Señora Cruz, I'm going to the Internet café in town. I'll be back in about an hour."

"Take your time," Señora Cruz called as Elena headed out. She walked toward the Internet café she'd seen in the *parte vieja*. She knew it would be cheaper to e-mail Claire from the multimedia center at school on Monday, but she couldn't

wait. She was so excited about her writing, and she knew Claire was the one person who would understand. Plus, she wanted to fill her in on Miguel.

To: dramagirl23@email.com
From: LanieH@email.com
Subject: tapas, not topless

Claire,

Well, we went to the tapas bars last night for the first time. (It sounds like topless bars if you say it fast, as my friend Alex pointed out.) But they aren't like that at all. They're these really fun, relaxed places where you serve yourself from rows and rows of plates on top of the bar. The whole thing was very social—you would have loved it!

I should probably also mention that I fell for a boy last night. His name is Miguel, and he's beautiful from every angle. Too bad he's after my friend Jenna. I guess I'll just have to admire him from afar—it's what I do best.

I really wish you were in this play production class with me. I just finished writing the first assignment, and I've never felt so excited about homework. In fact, it didn't feel like work at all. You know how people say that everyone has a talent, or something that they really love more than anything? I really think playwriting could be my thing. We have this contest in class where the groups who write the best two plays get to direct them and stage them for an audience. You know I'm

gunning for that. How awesome would that be?

Don't worry, I'm taking mad notes, and I'll share all the wis-dom with you when I get home.

Miss and love you!!

Elena

On her way home, Elena's encounter with Miguel the night before spun over and over through her head like a broken film reel. Even if he was interested in Jenna, she wished she would have been different. Next time she ran into him she would be prepared. It wasn't so hard to imagine herself daz-zling him with funny stories. In the film that played in her mind, she was charming, confident, and funny. She knew it was a long shot, but a girl could dream.

Elena had been excited all weekend about turning in her play assignment, but on Tuesday, during the break between Spanish and play production, she found herself in a deep funk. She slumped beside Jenna toward the fountain in the middle of the quad, which had unofficially become the meet-ing place for all of her friends.

"Don't worry about Señor Gonzalez. He's tough on every-one," Jenna soothed, linking her arm through Elena's. The gesture made Elena feel a little better. "He was such a jerk chewing you out in front of the class."

"It's just that I was so focused on my play assignment, I completely forgot about the Spanish homework."

"Don't stress about it."

"I'm just mad at myself," Elena lamented. "I was ready to be a new person here. I thought coming to a new place would bring out the best in me—help me focus. Now I'm supposed to turn this play assignment in, and I'm not even excited anymore.

The two girls passed a group of Spanish boys, and one of them stopped and said, *"Hola."*

"Hey, we know you. How's it going?" Jenna replied.

Elena looked up and found herself staring up at Miguel's hazel eyes, which actually looked almost green in the bright sunlight. Suddenly her problems with Señor Gonzalez seemed totally unimportant. She had fantasized about seeing him again, but she hadn't imagined it being so soon. Now that he was actually standing in front of her, she found herself practically mute, once again.

"Are you students here?" Miguel asked. "I did not realize."

"Yeah, we're in the International School program. I didn't know you were in high school. You look older," Jenna said.

Miguel smiled broadly. "No, I am seventeen."

"So, what do you do when you're not in school?" Jenna asked.

"I work at the Maria Cristina. It is a hotel; perhaps you've heard of it?" he said.

"Yeah, it's supposed to be pretty fancy, isn't it?"

Miguel nodded as one of his friends approached. Elena thought he looked familiar.

"This is my cousin, Borja." When Miguel said the name Borja, the r rolled off his tongue.

"Nice to meet you, Bor-ha," Elena said, her r falling flat instead of trilling off her tongue the way it had for Miguel. When Borja held his hand out to shake with Jenna, he dipped his head slightly, and Elena immediately realized why he looked familiar. It was the same hand-out pose and gentlemanly bow he had used when asking Jenna to dance the other night at the tapas bar. He was the curly-haired boy who'd had Jenna stomping to the flamenco music.

"Well, I guess we'll see you around," Jenna said as they scooted off toward their next classes "I can't believe we go to the same school," Jenna continued as soon as the boys had left. "We could see them every day."

Elena slipped into the classroom just as Ms. B began collecting assignments. Elena took a seat, leaned back in her chair, and stared out the window. She thought about how cute Miguel had looked squinting in the bright sunlight. Elena was still wrapped up in thoughts of Miguel when Ms. B appeared next to her desk. Smiling at Ms. B, she handed over her assignment without hesitation. She'd been so busy dreaming about Miguel that she had completely forgotten to be nervous.

Chapter Six

On Sunday afternoon Elena, Jenna, and Alex were enjoying what they had recently discovered was one of the purest pleasures in San Sebastián. When most of the town was enjoying siesta, they were slurping dribbles of melting ice cream as it rolled down their cones and onto their fingers.

They walked along the shaded walkway that hugged Río Urumea, the river that slithered through the core of the city, dividing the old section of town from the new.

"Here," Jenna said, shoving a tilting mess of ice cream under Elena's nose as they crossed one of the bridges that led back toward the center of town. "Try the pistachio."

They were on their way back from a small chunk of beach Alex had discovered called Playa de Zurriola. It was less well known than Playa de la Concha, but still beautiful. Zurriola, a field of white sand that lay at the foot of one of the green mountains, was considered to be a beach for locals and surfers. It was roomier than la Concha, and there was a nice view of the colorful houses that climbed up the side of the mountain. On their first trip to Zurriola earlier in the week, they discovered a friendly old man selling ice cream, *helado* in Spanish, out of a little cart. They'd sought him out again today strictly for the novelty of it.

On the other side of the bridge the three of them started up the tree-lined river walk, where they found an iron bench. They sat down to finish their messy cones. The city was hushed and sleepy, and the warm breeze was lulling Elena into a daze. She loved this time of day in Spain—when the air was the warmest and all the people strolled past each other, stopping to talk for a moment. She didn't miss the hectic afternoons back home, rushing to after-school activities or working frantically to finish a homework assignment. She didn't even think the Spanish had a word for hectic. If they did, she had yet to hear it.

"We get our first conflict assignments back tomorrow, Elena," Alex said, slurping a rogue drip from his cone. "How do you think you did?"

"I feel okay about it, I guess. But I'm impressed you know when we get our assignments back. I didn't know you stayed

awake long enough to hear that kind of thing," Elena teased.

"Well, I can't believe you remembered to turn in your assignment at all. I heard about your little slipup in Gonzalez's class."

"Hey," Elena shoved his shoulder, though Alex barely swayed against her skinny arms. "I told you this class is different. I'm really motivated. I swear."

"Relax, Holloway. I'm just teasing." Alex smirked at her. "So, Jenna, how's your architecture class going?" Elena couldn't help but notice that Alex softened his tone a little when he addressed Jenna.

"Pretty cool. We've been designing our dream house."

"I bet yours is sweet."

Jenna threw him a sly smile. "It's okay."

Alex crunched the last of his ice cream cone and stood up. "Well, it's been fun, but I've gotta go. I've got a test in Basque culture tomorrow. Later."

"Se ya," the two girls called after him.

Once Alex was out of earshot, Jenna perked up. "Are you sure you're not into him?"

"Yes. Absolutely, one-hundred percent sure." Elena licked her cone, turned it a little, then licked again. "He's all yours."

Jenna ignored the last comment. "He's not your type or what?"

Elena shook her head.

"Well, who *is* your type then? I'm curious. We've met boys

in school, at the tapas bars, all over. You must think someone is just the tiniest bit cute."

Elena shrugged. She hadn't told Jenna about Miguel.
She'd never been very open about her crushes, even though
the whole world seemed to find out about them anyway.

"Well, there is one person I think is pretty cute," Elena
ventured, but then rushed to qualify her statement. "He
would never even look in my direction, though, so it's not like
I'm expecting anything to happen."

Jenna sighed. "Give me a break, Elena. Who is it?"

"You know that Spanish guy we met at the tapas bar and
then ran into on campus the other day...."

"Which one? Miguel?" Jenna shrieked. Elena nodded and
tried to shush her friend, but Jenna barreled forward. "Oh,
yeah, he's hot. And seems so sweet," she added.

"Well, you never know," Elena said, remembering how
sincere Joe had seemed at first.

"You guys would be so cute together," Jenna continued
as she finished off her cone. "Oh my God, I have the best
idea." Jenna sprang up from the bench. "Follow me."

Jenna led Elena up a path that wound past a damp man-
icured lawn and around a massive brown stone building
with the words, HOTEL MARIA CRISTINA, scrolled in grand letters across the top.

"This is where Miguel works," Elena whispered.

"I know. I want to get started on getting you two together."

"Jenna, it's not me he's interested in," Elena protested.

"You've talked to the guy, like, twice for a total of five minutes. How would you know who he likes?"

Because it's obvious he likes you, Elena wanted to say. But she held back. She didn't want to lay it all out. Anyway, she was sure Jenna knew the effect she had on boys.

"Listen, if he's not here, we'll just check out the swanky hotel and leave," Jenna said frankly. "No big deal."

Elena was a little embarrassed to be hunting Miguel down at work, but also secretly excited. She could picture him looking gorgeous in his bellhop uniform, his tan skin set against the crisp white cotton. She would be poised, striding up to him with the grace of a dancer. "Hello." He'd beam. "I didn't think I'd see you again so soon. What a wonderful surprise." *Elena, you're hopeless,* she thought.

Elena followed Jenna through the canopied front entrance and into the gleaming lobby. They stood beneath a crystal chandelier, its light bouncing off the rosy marble floor. Jenna pulled Elena past the empty bar and idle grand piano toward the dining room. The windows stretched up tall and arcing to graze the ceiling. The molding at the top of the ceiling looked like cake frosting. When Elena glanced over her shoulder, she felt the eyes of the concierge burning into them. She suddenly felt out of place and antsy to leave.

Elena grabbed Jenna's hand and steered her back to the front of the lobby.

"He's obviously not here," she whispered, turning her head to look at Jenna. "That guy behind the desk is giving me the creeps and—" Before she could finish her sentence she felt herself smack into someone. When she turned her head, she found herself staring directly into Miguel's eyes. They were inches from her own. For a split second she thought, *If this boy ever kissed me, this is what it would feel like the moment before our lips touched.* She stepped back, adjusting the neckline of her shirt, which had slid off her shoulder on one side.

"I am so sorry," he said. "I hope I did not hurt either of you. I was not looking where I was going." Each word was like a carefully wrapped package. Elena thought his English was better than hers. He was so polite, so considerate. She knew she should say something, but nothing came.

"Miguel," Jenna's full voice ricocheted off the marble lobby. "It's so funny that we ran into you."

"Yes, funny," he said, glancing back at the creepy guy behind the desk.

"We were curious about the famous Maria Cristina, so we thought we'd take a look. We completely forgot that you work here."

He smiled meekly and pulled at his collar.

"I will work here for only one more year. Next fall I plan to go to university in Madrid," he added quickly. Then he puffed up a little. "What do you think of the Hotel Maria Cristina?"

"It's really pretty." Jenna nodded.

"Everything in this hotel is gorgeous," Elena said, and then thought, *Including you.*

"I wonder what the rooms are like," Jenna mused, leaning back to take in the ceiling. "I bet they're awesome."

Miguel glanced furtively over his shoulder again at the eagle-eye concierge who was speaking in hushed tones with a customer. "Would you like to see one?" he whispered. Both girls nodded vigorously.

Miguel quickly shuttled them over toward the tucked-away service staircase. They marched up a narrow flight of concrete stairs. Miguel held his hand against the small of Jenna's back to steady her on one of the steps.

When Miguel opened the door to the second-floor land-ing, they stepped back into the centuries-old grace of the hotel. He nodded to a woman with white hair like spun sugar worn in a coif on her head. She was dressed in a maid's uni-form. She whispered heavily to him in Spanish. When he glanced in the girls' direction and whispered something in return, the diminutive elderly maid giggled and then let him into the room she had just exited.

"This way," he said, waving them into the room. "*Gracias,* Celia." The older woman looked up at him with warm eyes and let out a giggle. She turned back down the hall, pushing her cart lined with towels, cleaning supplies, and little bot-tles of shampoo and lotion.

They walked into the room, and Jenna gasped on cue.

"This is amazing," she said, walking over to the burnished armoire. A gold chandelier hung from the center of the ceiling, dripping amber light over the silver-threaded bedcovers. Elena wondered if there was a chandelier in every room.

"I'm going to check out the bathroom," Jenna said. "Don't worry, Miguel. I won't touch anything." When Miguel turned away, Jenna winked at Elena, then disappeared into the bathroom. Elena looked at Miguel. She hoped he wouldn't be bored without Jenna in the room to entertain him.

Elena suddenly realized the awkwardness of her situation. She was standing alone in a hotel room with a cute boy she barely knew who made her want to melt.

"Would you like to be in the bed?" he asked.

"Um, excuse me?" She should have known he would have an ulterior motive for bringing them up to this room. He was cute, but come on. "Listen, I don't know what you had in mind, but—"

His face flushed. "Um. Like this?" He sat gingerly on the edge of the bed.

"Oh," she croaked, "you meant, do I want to *sit on* the bed?" She had taken his flawless English for granted.

He nodded, his eyes focused on the rug. Elena felt awful. She sat down beside him, which should have been innocent but was now tainted by their earlier misunderstanding. They sat in silence as he ran the toe of his shoe along the ridge of the rug and Elena watched the door to the bathroom praying for Jenna to come back out.

"Is there a view?" she asked suddenly. She was proud of herself for initiating conversation for once. She stood up and walked toward the glass doors that led to the balcony.

"Yes." He perked up. "There is a nice view from this room." He pulled open the doors and they walked out onto a semi-circular patio. "See, there is the Urumea River. And there is the beach." He stretched out, leaning over the lip of the stone rail and pointed, and then stepped back to let her look.

"Oh, I see it." She lit up. "Look, there's a little boat." She pointed to a white speck bobbing across the horizon.

He leaned in behind her to catch a glimpse of the lonely boat. He radiated a lovely boy smell of faint cologne, soap, and a hint of the ocean. "Do you like boats?"

She thought for a moment and then said, "I guess so. I haven't actually been on many boats."

"My father has a sailboat. I go sailing sometimes," he said, as he walked back into the room and she followed.

"Oh my God, you have a boat," Jenna screeched as she joined them in the room. "That is so cool."

"Well, I can take you sometime. We can go out next weekend, if you are available."

Jenna raised an eyebrow and looked at Elena. Elena nodded to show that she was interested.

"Saturday's good. I'm so impressed that you have a boat," Jenna said, nudging Miguel in the ribs. "Don't you think that's awesome, Elena?"

"Awesome." Elena nodded. Jenna looked at her for a

moment, perhaps willing her to say something more, but Elena's mind went blank.

"Well, it is, what is the word?" He closed his eyes to search the English side of his brain. "Uh, humble? And it is actually my father's."

Jenna worked out the details with Miguel as Elena stood by quietly. He seemed so nice. Elena reminded herself of what Gwen was always telling her about having too much faith in people right away.

"Elena," she'd say, "you can't give your heart away so quickly. That's the surest way to get it broken."

"I should get back downstairs," Miguel said finally.

"Yeah, we'd hate to get you in trouble," Elena said.

Miguel shut the patio doors, closed the curtains, and smoothed down the bedspread. On the way out he straightened the magazines on the desk even though no one had touched them. Elena smiled softly. She had almost done the same thing.

Miguel spirited them down the service staircase and then snuck them out of the lobby when he was sure the manager at the front desk was occupied.

Once Elena and Jenna had walked back outside, Jenna looped her arm through Elena's.

"You do like him, don't you?"

"Yeah, why?"

"I just never would have known if you hadn't told me. You barely said a word to him."

"Jenna, I don't think Miguel even cared that I was there," Elena said. "I think he made the boating date as a way to spend more time with *you*."

"No way." Jenna waved off the idea. "Enough boy talk. Let's go do some window-shopping."

Elena wondered if Jenna had brushed her suggestion off as easily as it seemed. It was hard for her to imagine anyone giving up Miguel so easily, especially someone like Jenna. And she couldn't tell if Jenna really thought Elena had any kind of chance with him. She was pretty sure Jenna was too nice to say, "Yeah you're right. He'd never be interested in you. What was I thinking?" Regardless, she appreciated Jenna's encouragement.

To: dramagirl23@email.com
From: LanieH@email.com
Subject: Boy update

Hi Claire,

How is your week going? I realized today that it's probably almost time for the back-to-school dance. You'll have to fill me in on all the good gossip.

Today my friend Jenna and I were over at the Maria Cristina, this fancy hotel in town, and we "accidentally" ran into Mr. Beautiful, a.k.a. Miguel. And guess what? He asked us to go out on his boat with him next weekend! I feel sort of conflicted about the trip. I'm excited about going out into the harbor because boats and the ocean seem to play such a huge role in the lives of the locals here. And I have to admit that I'm excited about spending time with Miguel. But, I'm not so thrilled about watching him flirt with Jenna all day.

Even though I feel like I don't have a chance with this guy, I really like being around him. I like the way my name sounds in his Spanish accent—the way it's probably supposed to sound. And the way he talks is really polite without sounding snooty. If nothing else, the trip will be a chance to stare at Miguel for a few hours, right? Oh, and to see San Sebastián from the ocean, of course.

I miss you. Write soon!

Love, E

To: LanieH@email.com
From: dramagirl23@email.com
Subject: The San Jose Blues

Hey Chica,

This Miguel guy sounds fabulous! I'm sorry to hear he likes your friend, though you might not be able to tell just from meeting him a couple of times. I think you should just relax about the boating trip. At the very least this guy is someone new to take your mind off Joe. You could have a great time.

Who knows, maybe he'll end up being a great friend. (And you know, sometimes friendship blooms into something more.)

School started a couple days ago. Don't worry, you're not missing much. It's all the same old people doing the same old things. Yesterday, when I was shopping for an outfit to wear to the back-to-school dance, I ran into your sister at the mall. Don't worry, I'll definitely fill you in on any dance gossip.

I'm glad to hear you like the playwriting class. Are you picking up any good acting tips? Be sure to pass them on to your poor friend Claire. On second thought, don't tell me about it. It will just make me more jealous than I already am. I really miss you, Elena. I wish you could have been with me for the first day back at school. It was strange not to have you around to gossip with. I miss you tons and tons.

Keep me posted on your exciting life in Spain!

Love, C

The next day was much like the one that preceded it—sunny but a little cool, with a soft breeze feathering the ocean. Elena had just sat down for the start of her play production class, but she was staring out the window and daydreaming about what it would be like if Miguel were her boyfriend. She imagined their sailing out to sea on his boat at sunset.

"Elena, please see me after class," Ms. B said in a hushed tone as she passed Elena's desk on her way to the front of the classroom, breaking Elena from her little midday fantasy.

Elena's heart thumped inside her chest. She wondered what she could possibly have done to warrant an after-class meeting with the teacher. She nudged Alex in the ribs, causing him to snort and scoot up in his chair.

"Ms. B wants to talk to me after class," she whispered.

"So?" he grumbled.

"So, that's not good," she tried her best to talk without moving her lips.

"How do you know it's not good?"

She cut her eyes at him. Was he kidding? Being called to speak with the teacher after class was never good.

"Relax, Elena. Teachers love kids like you." Alex yawned and squashed his hat down low over his eyes, slumping back down into the crook of his chair.

"Not really," Elena mumbled. Compared to Jeremy and Gwen, Elena always felt she was a disappointment to most of her teachers.

"I hope everyone did last night's reading." Ms. B set down her roll sheet and sorted through several play texts. "Now don't get frustrated if your writing is not up to these standards." She gave them all a thoughtful, I've-been-there smile. "If you're going to attempt something, no matter what it is, it's worth taking a look at the best in that field."

At least Elena had done the reading. Maybe she could dazzle Ms. B with her deep insights into the plot and characters, and perhaps whatever crime she had unwittingly

committed would be magically erased from her rap sheet.

"Can anyone tell me what some of the themes are in *The Seagull*?" she asked, tapping the front cover of the Chekhov play and settling down on the corner of her desk.

Elena had some ideas, but she hesitated. Before she could get her hand up, Dylan's arm darted into the air.

"Yes, Dylan."

"The pursuit of a meaningful life and an artist's role in life." Dylan sat up straight, knowing she'd said the right thing.

"Yes. Excellent," Ms. B beamed at Dylan.

Elena slunk down in her seat. Ms. B certainly wasn't like other teachers. She swore and acted out scenes from the plays they were reading for homework. As long as Elena stayed out of the way and under the radar, most teachers left her alone and gave her decent grades. But Elena had a feeling Ms. B loved kids like Dylan who were cool and sharply opinionated.

Elena wondered what it could be that set Ms. B against her. Maybe it was just that her conflict piece was so generally bad that Ms. B had given up on marking Elena's paper, and now she had to talk to her face-to-face in order to outline every mistake she'd made. She glanced at the clock as the second hand clunked along one centimeter at a time. This was going to be a long class.

"Okay, everyone, class is almost over. I can see you guys

squirming to get out of here," Ms. B joked, drawing a round of chuckles from the class. "But I wanted to remind you that I'll be giving you instructions for the final play assignment soon. Next week we're going to be forming groups for that project, so you should start thinking about who you want to work with. If you don't have partners lined up, that's okay. I can match you with someone. But you have the option to work with one or two people you feel comfortable with."

Elena glanced at Dylan. She was sure Dylan already had some brilliant ideas rattling around in her brain and wondered if she had already paired up with someone for the project. A girl like Dylan would have her choice of partners.

"Remember, I'll be picking the top two plays, which will be staged and performed at the end of the semester. This is a big deal, you guys. Not only will you bask in the glow of staging your art for the public and your classmates, which should be motivation enough," Ms. B paused dramatically, allowing them to picture the glory of it, "but you will also get a pass on the written final. In other words, an automatic A."

A round of whoops was loosed in the classroom. Coming from a teacher's mouth, there were few words sweeter than "automatic A."

Finally, class was over. Elena took her time shuffling papers and placing her books and binder in her backpack as Ms. B handed back the first assignments. It took a while because Ms. B had a comment for each student as he or she collected a graded paper and then passed through the door.

The last student collected his paper from Ms. B and then wandered out into the sunshine.

Finally, Ms. B looked up from the one remaining student paper, which Elena assumed was hers.

"Hi, Elena. Please sit."

Elena drew a chair up to the side of Ms. B's desk and sat down. She couldn't read Ms. B's expression. "I read your conflict dramatization," Ms. B said.

Elena quickly looked down at her lap.

"Elena, have you taken many writing classes?"

"Just regular classes at school. Is that what you mean?"

"Well, I guess so," Ms. B leaned back. "I'm just wondering where you learned to write like this."

What did she mean? How did she write, exactly? Why wasn't Ms. B just getting to the point? Tell me what I did wrong so I can fix it, Elena screamed inside her head.

"I guess I don't understand," Elena ventured.

"Elena, this is excellent work," Ms. B said, leaning forward across her desk and forcing Elena to meet her gaze. "Your abilities exceed most people your age. I was just wondering if you've taken extra classes in this area."

Elena was stunned silent. She looked at Ms. B and realized why she couldn't place Ms. B's expression earlier. Ms. B wasn't talking to Elena as a teacher; she was talking to her like a mentor.

"Thank you." Elena managed to force the words out of her mouth. "But I haven't taken any extra classes or anything."

"Well, you're a natural," Ms. B shot her a broad grin. "You do write on your own though, don't you?"

"I mess around sometimes, but I've never really finished anything." Elena felt as if she was confessing a secret. She'd always made up little stories. For a while she kept beginnings of screenplays in a journal, but she was always worried one of her brothers would find it.

"Well, I wanted to let you know you're heading in the right direction," Ms. B said, slipping back into teacher mode. Although her version of teacher mode was still pretty relaxed and cool. "This doesn't mean I don't think there are areas for improvement, especially if you're interested in winning one of the top spots among the final play assignments. I think you have a good chance, but this year's class is a particularly talented pool of students. You'll do well if you really focus on the comments I made at the end of your paper and work on making those changes."

Elena realized her shoulders were still so tense they were practically touching her ears. She let them fall and felt lighter than she had in days.

"Thanks, Ms. B."

Ms. B handed her the paper with her name in the corner. "You got an A, by the way, in case you hadn't already figured that out." Ms. B laughed. "Great job, Elena. Please come see me if you have any questions along the way."

"I will," Elena nodded vigorously. She gawked at the A written in bold red ink, and the tight slanted letters just

below it that spelled out, *Excellent work!!!* She'd never been singled out in school before. Jeremy was the stellar student among her siblings, not under-the-radar Elena.

"Thanks a lot for the encouragement, Ms. B. I'll definitely take the final project seriously and work hard. I can't wait to get started." She knew she sounded like sort of a kiss-up, but she didn't care. Her words were sincere.

She grabbed her backpack from the floor, and slipped the straps over her shoulders. "See you in class tomorrow," Elena called.

"See you then, Elena," Ms. B returned. "And just because we had this little talk doesn't mean I'm going to go easy on you." Ms. B cocked her head to the side and grinned. "I'm going to hold you to a higher standard now. Don't disappoint me."

Elena nodded. Although Ms. B's words probably should have made her nervous, instead they stirred something in her that made her want to prove herself even more. It was as though a part of herself that had always been there was just waking up from a long hibernation.

Chapter Seven

"You should take a jacket," Señor Cruz called in Spanish from his spot on the couch as Elena hustled past him toward the front door. She was on her way to meet Jenna and Miguel for their boat outing. She was full of nerves and jittery excitement about the prospect of spending an afternoon on the water with Miguel.

Elena stopped in front of Señor Cruz. "The only jacket I have is a wool peacoat," she said.

"No, no. That won't do. You need something lightweight that will keep the water off." He pulled himself off the couch

and walked over to the hall closet. "Here. This is perfect." He held out a sleek black jacket. "This is Señora Cruz's. She won't mind if you borrow it for the afternoon."

Elena took the coat from Señor Cruz and tried it on. It fit amazingly well, and nipped in a little at the waist.

"*Muchas gracias*, Señor Cruz."

"Just remember to keep down whenever the boom comes around. You don't want to get knocked in the head."

She promised she would be careful and suddenly felt as if she was home, promising her own parents that she would be safe and follow all their instructions. She guessed parents were parents everywhere, but she appreciated Señor Cruz's concern.

"*Adios*, Señor," she called as she headed out the door and turned down the street toward the marina.

Elena ran into Jenna on her way to the harbor.

"Cute jacket," Jenna said, giving the hem a tug.

"It's Señora Cruz's."

"Not that you're going to need it, though," Jenna said, glancing up at the blue sky. "Hey, there he is. In front of the boat launch at eleven A.M. exactly." Jenna lowered her voice. "He's a man of his word. Now, what's cuter than that?"

"*Hola,*" Miguel said as the girls approached. "Elena and Jenna, do you remember my cousin, Borja?"

The girls said hello.

"Follow me," Miguel instructed. Elena, Jenna, and Borja

trailed him across the dock. Elena could see water sloshing through the wooden slats below their feet.

"Here she is," Miguel declared, stopping in front of a sailboat with the words LA MARIANA in meticulously stenciled letters across the back. The letters were so slick and vivid it looked as though it had been touched up only days earlier. That was the extent of the boat's painstaking care. The bulk of the vessel was rough and worn. The faded white paint was chipped in places, and fingers of rust stretched out across the metal piping. It was exactly how Miguel had described it—humble.

"Please get in," Miguel offered as he set about unwinding the ropes from their moorings. Borja stepped in first and turned toward Jenna.

"Tenga cuidado, amiga," he warned, pointing to the rocking rim of the boat. Borja held his hand out for Jenna to grasp as she wobbled onto the boat.

Elena climbed into the boat unassisted while Miguel handed out life vests, and began to run through some instructions. The only one Elena really paid attention to was the one that echoed what Señor Cruz had said about ducking from the heavy metal boom as it swung around to the other side of the boat any time Miguel said "Down."

Miguel joined them in the belly of the boat, and within minutes he had maneuvered the boat through the marina and they were tacking across the bay. Elena turned her back

to the wind and watched the retreating harbor, where colorful sailboats lofted on the waves. Behind the boats stood a
row of centuries-old apartment buildings built into the side
of the mountain, rising up behind all of it.

"Okay, now, everyone down," Miguel hollered over the
sound of the waves. Elena got a spray of seawater in her face
just before she bent down. She leaned as far down as she
could so that her face was almost even with her feet in the
damp floor of the vessel. She wasn't taking any chances.

"You can sit up now." Miguel laughed, yanking her up
playfully by the nylon strap of her life vest. "You really haven't
been on many sailboats, have you? You're funny." Borja and
Jenna chuckled, too. Jenna winked at her as if to say this
was a good sign, though Elena wasn't sure being the clown
was the best way to win a guy's heart.

They cruised across the calm bay. Miguel maneuvered
them deftly around two other boats, one smaller and the
other larger than LA MARIANA. Elena was starting to get the
appeal of this tattered little boat. It was weathered but sturdy.
Miguel seemed to know its every creak and groan.

"This is great," Jenna called over the waves and wind.
"I've always loved to sail. My family went on vacation once in
Florida," she told the boys. "My dad took us out on the ocean
a few times. This is a prettier view, though."

"What about you, Elena?" Miguel asked. "What do you
think of sailing so far?"

Elena pondered the question and let herself bob with the

boat as the waves rolled beneath them. "I never knew such a bumpy ride could be so relaxing," she said finally.

"Exactly," Miguel laughed. "You do not say much, Elena, but when you do, it is just the right thing."

Elena had never received such a strange compliment, but she felt herself glowing.

"My father always says it is a waste to use too many words when just a few will do," Miguel said, flashing Elena a broad smile. It was not a flirtatious smile, but it was open and friendly.

"You're a great sailor, Miguel," Jenna said. She looked genuinely impressed. "How long have you been sailing?"

"As long as I can remember. My father started taking me out at a young age. I was so young I could barely see over this." He gestured toward the side of the boat.

Miguel brought them around the small island situated in the center of the bay, which he told them was called la isla de Santa Clara. Up close Elena could see clusters of houses clinging to the land. She was surprised that people lived out there. There was something very romantic about the idea of living on an island that was so close to town, yet still separated by a rolling body of water.

"I sail, too," Borja volunteered in English that was mangled by a thick accent. He stole a glance at Jenna to see if she was impressed. "I used to have boat. I am a great sailor."

"Well, you'll have to take us out next time." Jenna smiled.

"It's true. Borja is a better sailor than me," Miguel admitted. "But my English is better."

Borja laughed at this. "Yes. Better English."

"Do you know Spanish very well?" Miguel asked them.

"We're taking classes. I'm not really a language person—math's my thing," Jenna said. Miguel nodded and then looked at Elena expectantly.

"Well," she hedged. "I really love Spanish. It's one of my favorite classes...."

"You must be good then." He smiled.

"Actually," she looked out at the rolling ocean just beyond the bay and wondered how far out they would be going. "Actually, I'm a little bit shy about speaking Spanish. I've had a few, mostly one-sided conversations with my host family. But when I speak with strangers, I just clam up."

"That can be a problem." Miguel nodded. "Down!" he shouted in Spanish.

They all ducked as the boom swung around again.

"I was saying that can be a problem," Miguel continued, "because many of the people here don't speak English. They speak Basque and Spanish, but not a lot of English."

"So I've noticed," Elena returned.

"We will have to work on your Spanish."

Elena waited for him to continue, but he was quiet as he looked up and noticed a flock of heavy clouds spreading rapidly across the sky. "We should watch those. They could mean a storm is coming."

"Are you kidding? It's beautiful out. Don't turn back yet," Jenna protested.

They were drifting out toward the choppy dark water of the open sea. Elena clung to the bench and held tight as they bounced over several larger waves. Salt water stung her eyes, and her arms began to cramp from gripping so tightly.

"So, who is Mariana?" Jenna asked.

"My father named this boat for my mother."

"She must be really flattered," Elena offered.

There was a long silence as Miguel fidgeted with one of the ropes. Borja looked out to sea.

"I'm sure she was," Miguel finally answered. "She died when I was three."

"I'm so sorry," Jenna said. Elena didn't know what to say. She felt so sad for him.

"I don't know much about her," Miguel continued in an even tone. "My father, how do I explain? Spanish men don't show those kinds of emotions, so he never talked about her very much. I do know that she was beautiful and she loved the ocean."

"Is that why you like to come out here so much?" Elena asked, without realizing what a nosy question it was until after she asked it.

"Yes, I think so." He nodded thoughtfully. When his head bobbed up, she stole a glance at his solemn expression. She realized that he wasn't just a perfect guy born from her imagination, but a real person with sadness and flaws.

Miguel took the boat headlong into the ocean. They were shuttling up, over, and down in the steady waves when the

sky suddenly darkened, and the clouds opened up. Rain came jetting down over them in ripping streams. This wasn't just a light rain. This was a storm, and they were far from shore. The city was just a shimmering line on the horizon.

Miguel took control of the sails and began shouting instructions in Spanish to Borja. Elena bowed her head in her lap. The Spanish word for down had washed away in her mind, and she didn't want to be caught with her head up when the boom swung around. She just wrapped her arms around her knees and tried to hold on as walls of water crashed into the side of LA MARIANA, knocking it sideways.

After a sheet of water covered their boat for the third time in as many minutes, Elena lifted her head a bit to ask Miguel if he thought he could really get them back safely. She could feel the fear rising up in her chest. But when she looked up and searched Miguel's face, she could have sworn he wore the trace of a smile. He looked completely absorbed and in his element. He looked as if he felt the way she had when she'd written her first play assignment, as if the whole world could drop away and nothing would matter as long as he was still doing what he was doing right now. She couldn't decide if this frightened or impressed her.

Finally, Miguel steered them into the bay. The rain let up for a few minutes, allowing them to sneak back into the boat's slip in the harbor. By the time they had tied the boat to the moorings and squeezed the rainwater from their clothes, the clouds were parting to reveal a bright sky. It almost looked as if the storm had never happened at all.

"Thank you so much for taking us out," Elena said as Borja and Miguel walked the girls out toward the road.

"De nada," Miguel said. "It was my pleasure." He seemed to consider each word before he spoke it, the way Elena did when she was trying to speak Spanish. "I hope to see you on campus." Miguel waved as the girls turned right and the boys headed in the opposite direction.

"You will," Jenna called. Then she nudged Elena in the arm and whispered, "I promise we'll see them again."

The next afternoon, Alita and Elena were sitting at the kitchen table working on their homework when she got a phone call from her family.

"Hi, honey," her mom said. "We miss you."

She never thought she'd be so happy to hear her mom's voice. "I miss you guys, too," Elena sighed, settling back into a chair at the table. "What's going on there?"

"Well, the back-to-school dance was last Friday. Gwen went with a big group of friends. Let's see, what else? Caleb has a new band—they play punk music, I think. He gets mad because I always call it the wrong thing."

Elena laughed.

"Have you contacted your great-aunt yet?"

"Not yet, Mom. I've just been so busy."

"Elena, please don't wait too long to make plans."

"I know. I won't, Mom." Elena breathed out sharply.

"Well, Jeremy's here. He wants to talk to you. Hold on."

There was a scratching sound as Elena's mom passed the phone to Jeremy.

"Hey, Lanie," Jeremy's voice boomed through the receiver.

"Hi, Jeremy. What's up?"

"Not much. I'm just starting to pack. I'm heading back to L.A. next weekend," he said. "What about you? Is Mom still bugging you about visiting Aunt Elena?"

"Yeah, but she doesn't really have to pressure me. I want to go. It's just that I'm still getting used to San Sebastián—I don't feel like I'm ready to head off to Barcelona yet, you know?" There was a barely discernible pause as Elena's voice rippled over an ocean and a continent to Jeremy's ears.

"Totally. I've heard Barcelona is awesome, though."

"Yeah. Me, too."

"And I think Great-Aunt Elena is pretty cool. I mean, I sort of remember her."

"What do you mean?"

"She visited Mom when I was in kindergarten."

"She did?"

"Yeah. You were *really* little, obviously. I don't remember much about her, but I know I thought she was really fun. She would get down on the ground and play with me. And I remember spending hours drawing with her. I think she's some kind of artist or something."

"What, like a painter?" Elena had always thought she was the only one in her family with any artistic impulses.

"Uh-huh. Actually, I think she might be sort of famous. Well, famous in Barcelona anyway."

"Hmm. Sounds interesting." She wondered why her mom hadn't mentioned her aunt's painting. Elena was definitely more intrigued by her now.

"Yeah. Hey, Gwen's bugging me to hand the phone over," Jeremy said. "I'll talk to you later."

Jeremy handed the phone to Gwen, and she immediately began filling Elena in on the back-to-school dance. Then Elena gave Gwen the rundown on Jenna, Alex, and all her new friends in Spain. She even managed to slip Miguel's name into the conversation, but she tried to keep her voice even and casual, to play it off as if he was just some guy she'd met. Gwen wasn't buying it.

"Oh my God, you love him," Gwen blurted.

"I do not," Elena insisted. "I just like him a tiny bit, hardly at all actually."

"Since when do you like someone a tiny bit? What about Robbie Bowers back in seventh grade? The first day of school you came home and told us all that you had met the love of your life. The first day you met him!"

"This is different," Elena insisted.

"And what about Mark Dorian in ninth grade?" Gwen plowed forward. "Not to mention Joe Cipriani last year."

"I've turned over a new leaf here. And I know what you're

going to say—don't fall in love before you even know the guy."

"That's exactly what I was going to say."

"It doesn't matter anyway because he's not interested."

"How do you know that?" Gwen sounded skeptical.

Elena filled Gwen in on her first encounter with Miguel at the tapas bar.

"He walked up and started to talk to me, but as soon as Jenna introduced herself I practically disappeared. It was so obvious he was after her all along."

"It just sounds like Jenna's a flirt."

"Also," Elena continued, "when we went to visit him at the hotel where he works, he kept finding reasons to touch Jenna's arm or her waist, like when he held his hand out to help her on the stairs."

Gwen laughed. "Maybe she needed help. Elena, I think you should just try to get to know this guy better before you rush to judgment either way," Gwen said, slipping into big sister mode. It was easy for Gwen to say; she was cool and rational by nature. Elena's world was colored by her emotions.

"I should get going," Gwen said finally. "You know how Dad is about the phone bill."

"Okay," Elena croaked. "Call again soon."

It was good to hear the voices of her family, but after every other time she had hung up, she'd spent the rest of the day with a dull sadness pressing into her chest.

Gwen seemed to sense her emotion. "Elena, you're in Spain. Stop thinking about us, and go enjoy it."

• • •

Elena was having trouble concentrating as Señor Gonzalez scratched illegible verbs on the board and called on students at random to conjugate them. It was the deadline for choosing partners in Ms. B's class, and Elena still didn't have one. Sometime since her meeting with Ms. B, Elena had become convinced that Dylan was the only partner who could help produce a winning play. Dylan would provide the edgy darkness, and Elena would bring the light and romance. Elena thought they were playwriting soul mates—a creative yin and yang. But she still hadn't gathered up the courage to ask Dylan to be her partner. She squirmed in her seat, antsy for the bell to ring so she could race to class and wait for Dylan. Elena had only a fifteen-minute break between classes to track her down. She couldn't believe she'd procrastinated so long.

"El-e-na Hol-lo-way." Señor Gonzalez's voice brought her back to the present. The stretched, irritated way he said her name let her know it was probably the second or third time he'd called it out.

"Um, yes?" she stammered.

All the eyes in the classroom were turned, waiting for her to fall flat on her face.

"Please conjugate the word *soñar* in the present tense."

She'd lucked out. She knew this one. *"Sueño, sueñas, sueña, soñamos, soñáis, sueñan,"* she recited confidently.

"And it means?"

"To dream."

For the rest of the class, Elena tried her best to pay attention. She'd narrowly escaped embarrassment, but she knew if
she continued to drift in class she wouldn't be so lucky.

By the time the bell finally rang to signal the end of class,
Señor Gonzalez had his students waiting silently at their
desks with their hands folded and their bags packed. Elena
decided he must have served in the Spanish army. He had
every class planned out like a boot camp schedule. It was
always such a stark contrast moving from his regimented
classroom to the freely flowing creativity in Ms. B's class.

The bell rang, and Elena darted out of the classroom and
began to charge across the quad toward the campus theater, where Ms. B would be holding class for the day. She
kept an eye on the theater entrance so she could catch
Dylan on her way inside.

"Elena," she heard her name ring out behind her. When
she turned she found Alex sitting on the grass in the quad.
"Whoa, slow down, man. Are you in a race or something?" he
called, hoisting himself up and slumping toward her at his
usual pace, as if the world would wait for him. "I was hoping
to catch you on your way to the theater."

"You were?" She tipped her head to the side to steal a
look at the theater door. No sign of Dylan yet. "What's up?"

"Wanna walk together?"

"Uh, okay. But I'm kind of in a hurry."

Alex shrugged and ambled along beside her. Apparently

"hurry" was not in his vocabulary, along with "stress," she imagined.

"How was Spanish?" Alex asked.

"Just the usual, conjugating verbs and stuff."

"Uh, you know how we're supposed to pair up for the final play thing in Ms. B's class today?" Alex asked.

"Uh-huh," she nodded. She kept her eyes trained on the theater door as they approached.

"Well, um, what do you think about you and me?" he asked, kicking at an overgrown tuft of grass that was springing from a crack in the walkway.

"What do I think about you and me?" She repeated, slowing down and searching his face, which she could actually see for once because he had yanked off his hat and was raking his hands through his sun-bleached hair. It was particularly scruffy today, as though he'd been surfing instead of going to his morning classes and hadn't had time to shower before finally showing up for school. He definitely took advantage of the loose attendance rules at the International School. She had once heard Ms. B give him a lecture about how I.S. was like college in that each student was responsible for his own success.

"Yeah, you know. What do you think about the two of us being partners for the final project?"

Elena's throat tightened. Why hadn't she seen this coming? "Um, wow," she stammered. "I hadn't really thought about it, to be honest."

"Really? But, we have to choose our partners by today." He put his hat back on his head and slid the bill down to shade his eyes. It did seem ridiculous that she wouldn't have given it any thought until that moment. For some reason she couldn't tell him that she was planning to ask Dylan to be her partner.

"Come on, Elena." He laughed. "It's not like I'm asking you to the prom or anything. It's just a play."

Just a play? This was exactly why she hadn't thought of Alex as a viable partner. He didn't take anything seriously, and this was very serious to her. In the distance she saw Dylan approaching the theater along with a purple-haired boy wearing a Sex Pistols T-shirt. This was Elena's chance.

"Listen, Elena," Alex said grasping her shoulder and stopping them in the middle of the walkway. "If you don't want to be partners—that's cool. I just think we'd make an awesome team. I think we'd, like, balance each other out." He let go of her arm and stepped back. His face was a question mark.

She glanced back at the door in time to see Dylan laughing at something the purple-haired boy had said. She suddenly realized why she couldn't tell Alex about Dylan. Elena hadn't even said more than two words to her since she'd hatched this plan to pair up with her for the project. Who was she kidding? Alex was her friend; he was literally the first friend she'd made in Spain. He was the obvious choice, the only choice really, since she didn't know anyone else in class very well. Including Dylan.

"You're right, Alex." She nodded, matter-of-factly. "We would balance each other out."

"So, it's a deal?"

"Yeah." She smiled. "We can be partners for the project."

"Cool."

Elena began to pass through the door to the theater, but she could feel that Alex wasn't following her. She turned around to face him.

"Uh, so you'll just tell Ms. B that we're gonna be partners, right?" He was retreating from the classroom slowly like a wild animal edging away from a cage.

"You aren't coming in?"

He looked over his shoulder at the opposite row of classrooms, but she knew he saw through the classrooms and the buildings beyond them to the ocean breaking on the beach. "Um, it's just that the waves are really awesome today," he answered. She halfheartedly understood—the ocean was calling him.

"Yeah, sure. I'll tell her," she sighed.

"Thanks, Elena. We'll get together over the weekend to start working, okay?"

She waved him off, stepped inside the theater, and slunk into a seat. Resting her head in her palm, she watched Alex retreating back through the open door and wondered what she had gotten herself into.

Chapter Eight

"Sorry I'm late," Elena said one afternoon a couple weeks later as she slid into a seat at the outdoor table with Jenna and Marci. The girls had planned to meet at their new favorite café on Alameda del Boulevard, a wide tree-lined street, and Elena was late as usual. They'd come under the premise of studying, but it looked as though Marci and Jenna hadn't even taken their books out of their backpacks yet.

"No problem," Marci said, pushing a *café con leche* across the table. "We ordered this for you."

"Thanks. Where's Caitlin?"

"Her horticulture class has an all-day field trip."

Elena nodded. "So, what's up?"

"I was just saying we should plan a road trip." Jenna took a sip of her coffee, then licked a dab of foam from her upper lip. "I just think, you know, we have two more months in Spain, so we should see as much variety as we can."

"The school has a trip to Bilbao," Elena offered, stirring three sugars into her cup. She had become a big fan of coffee since Señora Cruz introduced her to it on her first morning in Spain. Elena counted it as a way to absorb some European culture. People here loved their strong coffee. "I think the Bilbao trip includes a tour of the Guggenheim Museum."

"I'm not talking about a school trip to a stuffy museum." Jenna sighed. "I'm talking about a fun road trip with just our friends."

A waiter came by their table, and Elena and Jenna ordered *churros con chocolate* with their coffee.

"I'll have a bottled water, too," Elena said as the waiter was leaving their table. He asked her something that sounded like, "With a glass?" She nodded. A glass would be nice.

"Okay, Jenna, where do you think we should go?" Elena asked.

"Well, I was talking to this guy in my Basque culture class, and he told me about a place called Ibiza." Jenna leaned forward in her chair. "It's this tiny island off the coast of Barcelona where people go clubbing all night and then sleep on the beach all day."

"I thought you wanted to see the variety of Spain?" Elena asked. "That doesn't sound so different from being here except for maybe a few more parties."

"It would be cool to see some more culture, like a big museum or a festival," Marci agreed. "This Ibiza place sounds sort of small and out of the way."

"Well, yeah. That's the whole point." Jenna tossed her arms up and fell back in her chair. "Small and out of the way means *cool*."

The girls sat in silence for a moment. Elena watched as a group of older Spanish men dressed in linen suits settled at a table nearby and began a card game. Elena loved that the Spanish people made a point of dressing to go out, even if it was just to a café around the corner.

The waiter returned with their order. Marci refused to eat deep-fried sticks of bread that were rolled in sugar, but Elena didn't think twice about dunking the crispy-chewy batons of sweet bread in chocolate and devouring them blissfully. Elena noted that the waiter hadn't brought her a glass and that the water was fizzy. She wasn't in the mood to send it back, so she took a sip. It was like Coke with all the taste removed. Yuck. Who drinks plain carbonated water?

Elena pushed the water aside then dug through her backpack to see if she had anything else to drink. Her hands traced the spine of her mom's Spanish tour book. Elena had thrown it in there weeks ago and had nearly forgotten about it.

"So, we agree that Jenna's idea of a road trip is a good one, right?" Elena began diplomatically as she slapped the guidebook on the iron tabletop and leafed through the flimsy pages. The two girls agreed. "Jenna wants to have an adventure, and Marci would like to see a museum."

"What do you want to do?" Jenna asked Elena.

Elena pressed her fingers against her lips, thinking. "Actually, I'd really love to see some flamenco dancing."

Elena passed the book to Marci, who flipped to the front and scanned through the list of Spanish cities. "What about a weekend in Madrid?" Marci asked.

"Everyone's going to go to Madrid." Jenna pouted. "It's so obvious."

"Exactly," Marci countered, finding the section on Madrid and sliding the book toward Jenna. "It's so obvious that we should definitely see it. It's a huge city. It has everything we're looking for: museums, discos, shopping..."

Elena had to admit that Marci made a good case. Even Jenna had hushed. She had her nose pressed into the section highlighting Madrid.

"Oooh," Jenna cried, stopping at a bright picture of a matador trimmed in gold braid, swirling a red cape, "We could see a bullfight. We should get a big group together for this, you guys."

"Someone should probably be in charge of organizing it, if it's going to be big," Marci suggested.

"Not it," Elena called. "I mean, I'll help out, but I shouldn't be in charge."

"I'll plan it," Jenna took another slug of her coffee, emptying her cup. With caffeine charging through her bloodstream, Jenna began flipping through the Bible-thin pages more furiously. "There can't be that much to it."

"Well, you'll have to figure out who's going and how much everyone is willing to pay for hotels and stuff," Marci offered.

"And then there's the question of how to get there," Elena said. "And I think they only have bullfights on certain days."

"You're right. And maybe we should see if Alex and Chris want to come, too."

"Good idea," Elena said. She had almost added that they should invite the boys along, but realized that Jenna was probably already thinking of that.

Elena pulled her Spanish textbook out of her backpack, setting it on the table. "What do you think, should we get started on Spanish?"

"I guess." Jenna slumped forward.

The girls studied for a while, until the sun began to set over the ocean. Elena loved that she could order something small at a Spanish café and then lounge there for hours without someone rushing to get her away from the table.

"I have to go, you guys. I told Señora Cruz I'd be home by sundown." Elena shoved her chair out with a scrape and picked her backpack up off the ground. "This Madrid idea sounds fun. We should talk about it again at school this week. I'll invite Alex, and I'll help you with the planning, J."

"Thanks," Jenna returned.

Elena waved good-bye to the two girls and headed up the Paseo de la Concha. She stopped for a breath, leaning against the white iron railing as she watched a group of boys starting a spontaneous game of soccer, or *fútbol*, as it was called in Europe. Before coming to Spain she'd never really noticed the beautiful simplicity of the game. Anyone could start up a spontaneous game of *fútbol*, and they often did, as long as they could round up something to kick and a few people willing to run around in the sun for an hour.

Elena started back up the avenue. Now that it was October, the air was getting cooler and the sun was beginning to set earlier in the evening. That didn't seem to stop packs of locals from enjoying the evening *paseo*, though. Elena ambled with the throng, taking her time getting back to the Cruz apartment.

When she got home, Señora and Alita were sitting at the table chatting.

"How was your studying date?" Señora Cruz asked in Spanish.

"Bien, gracias," Elena said, plunking down on the couch. Señora Cruz settled into the chair opposite her.

"How is Jenna?" Alita asked, sitting next to Elena on the couch. "Tell her to come and visit us soon. We miss her."

"I'll tell her," Elena promised. "She's fine. She came up with her latest plan for an adventure."

Señora Cruz chuckled. "What does she have in mind now?"

"Well, we're thinking of taking a weekend trip to Madrid." Elena stole a glance at Señora Cruz to gauge her immediate reaction.

"That's a wonderful idea. Madrid is a fascinating city."

"Can I come with you?" Alita begged, clinging to Elena's arm. "I can be your guide. We were there last year."

"Alita, you can go with your own friends when you're older." Señora Cruz hopped up from the chair and began digging through the hall closet until she produced a photo album. "We were there for a month last year."

"A month. Why so long?"

"It was our vacation."

"Wow, that's a long time for a vacation. My family vacation last year was a weeklong trip to Lake Tahoe."

"Spanish people take at least a month for holiday. It is common." Señora Cruz sat down on the other side of Elena and opened the leather cover of the album. "Here we are at the Puerta del Sol. You should definitely see this."

Alita leaned in to inspect a photo of herself in front of a fountain.

"So you don't have a problem with my going to Madrid for the weekend?" Elena prodded.

"As long as your parents say it is all right, and you are going with a group of friends, I think it would be a good experience."

Elena smiled and looked back at the album. She was pretty sure her mom would be okay with the trip since she was the one trying to get Elena to go to Barcelona by herself.

She was nervous about going to such a big foreign city, but as long as she had her friends with her she was pretty sure she couldn't do anything too spacey like getting lost on the subway or misplacing her passport. Although she wasn't entirely convinced....

Although Elena and Alex had planned to meet a couple weekends earlier to start working on their final play assignment, Alex had flaked because the waves were so good. Then he flaked again several more times during the week. Elena had suggested meeting at the library each time. Finally, Alex explained that the library was just too constricting. He suggested they meet in the late afternoon the following Friday at the top of Monte Igueldo, the mountain that stood across the bay from Monte Urgull. Alex claimed the expansive view from the summit would serve as inspiration.

There was a walking path that led to the top of the mountain, but Elena took the funicular instead. Mostly because she was curious to see what a funicular was. She found that it was really just a rickety train car. The thing that made it a

funicular and not a mere train was the fact that it was tugged by a cable up the mountainside. She climbed aboard and let the cliff-climbing train lurch her toward the summit. The funicular was slow, but it was easier than walking. The Cruzes were always telling her to walk everywhere. "It is only a ten-minute walk; it is good for you," they would say. She had begun to notice that to the Cruzes, everything was a ten-minute walk—whether it actually took five minutes or a half hour.

Elena disembarked the funicular at a circular track at the top of the mountain. The paved platform spread out to the edges of cliffs that were hedged in by short cement barriers. She could see immediately that there was a panoramic view of the entire city, and beyond.

"Wow," Elena exclaimed as she walked up to Alex, who was staring out at the ocean. "This view is amazing."

"Isn't it awesome?" He peered over the ledge with her.

From Monte Igueldo's perspective, her usual view of San Sebastián was inverted. Instead of floating out in the distance, Santa Clara Island sat just beyond her reach. Beyond the humpback of the island lay the ocean-front buildings, and above them stood the oversized ivory statue of Jesus watching over everything from its perch on top of Monte Urgull. Stretched back even farther was the gentle upward slope of town and even more mountains beyond it, crowned with lavender strips of clouds.

"Okay, you were right," Elena acknowledged. "If we aren't inspired here, then we won't be inspired anywhere."

"Told ya." Alex smiled. He took pride in knowing the landscape as well as any local. He was constantly exploring, seeking a location more interesting or beautiful than the last.

They laid out a blanket and settled onto the ground, and Elena dug through her backpack, pulling out a notebook filled with story sketches. After her encouraging meeting with Ms. B a few weeks before, she'd begun collecting ideas as they surfaced in her mind. Alex didn't appear to have a backpack with him, or even a sheet of paper or a pencil.

"Okay, why don't we get started," she suggested. "I wrote down some ideas. Did you brainstorm anything?"

"I told you, Elena, my ideas come to me spontaneously. My idea factory never lets me down," he said, tapping on his forehead.

"Okay, why don't you switch that idea factory into high gear and show me what it can do," she challenged.

"Well, Ms. B wants us to write about teenagers and what they care about, right?" He stretched out on his belly and propped his head in his hands.

"Right."

"Okay, let's think about it. What are our issues?"

She flipped to one of the pages where she'd written a few of the hurdles she and some of her friends had dealt with the previous school year. "Well, I was thinking we could write

about someone's parents getting divorced, or a kid who gets messed up on drugs, or maybe, like, an abusive relationship."

"Yeah, the drug thing is good." Alex nodded. "But everyone talks about the time they almost ODed."

"They do?"

"Yeah."

"*Who* talks about that?" Elena didn't know anyone who'd overdosed on anything.

"Come on, Elena. Everyone has their 'I almost ODed this one time' story," he continued, as if this were common knowledge. "I just think everyone in that class is going to write about those things. We should set ourselves apart."

"Set ourselves apart?" She couldn't believe what she was hearing. Alex was splayed across the ground with eyes so heavy-lidded he looked as if he was almost asleep. And yet there was a spark of competitive spirit somewhere deep within.

"Yeah, I mean, you want to be picked for one of the final performances, don't you?"

"Definitely."

"So think about it." He scrambled up into a sitting position. She could practically see the synapses in his brain firing to life. "What makes kids do all those messed-up things?"

Elena shrugged. She didn't understand how this was going to set them apart, but she was willing to see where Alex was heading with this.

"They're just trying to find their place, you know? Figure

out who they are and where they belong, right?"

Was that right? she wondered. It couldn't possibly be that simple, and yet there was something about it that resonated.

"Maybe it should be about a journey." Alex squinted out at the blue Bay of Biscay, but he seemed to be concentrating on something more elusive.

"A journey where?" she prodded.

Alex scrunched his forehead down so that the skin between his eyes folded into deep ridges. "Maybe a journey by someone who's adopted and is looking for his real mom," Alex cried, sitting up quickly, his eyes shining.

Elena had never seen him so animated. "That's good. Maybe he's always had questions about who he really is, and where he belongs," she continued, feeding off his energy, "and he thinks finding his roots will be the answer."

"He should meet some interesting characters along the way."

Elena nodded, encouraging him to continue.

"Maybe some of them knew his mom. He's, like, putting together this puzzle of who he is while he's also getting closer to finding her."

"Maybe he meets a girl," Elena said. She was a sucker for a love story. "She could be, like, a real free-spirit, wanderer type."

"Yeah, yeah. He's from the 'burbs and he's really sheltered, and she's a city girl who helps him navigate the streets."

They continued to bat ideas around, and Elena scribbled

them all down. With every suggestion Alex tossed out, Elena had one of her own to add. They were building off of each other's momentum. It reminded her of the times she'd listened to Caleb's band jamming in their garage. The guys would start out wailing on their instruments, stirring a jumble of noise. But eventually someone would pick out a melody and each instrument would fall in line with it, building on what the other had formed and creating something whole and unique.

"This is going to be a great road-trip story," she said after they had been working for a while.

"Yeah," Alex nodded. "But in the end, it'll really be about him finding his way home. Every good journey story is about finding your way home, don't you think? Like Odysseus in *The Odyssey*." Elena didn't answer but stared, mouth agape. Who was this guy and what had he done with the Alex she knew who slept through most of his classes and spent every spare moment exploring or catching waves?

By the time the sun was setting, Alex's manic energy had begun to wane. He leaned back on the blanket, propping himself on his elbows.

"Well, I think we've got some great stuff so far," he said.

"Next time we meet we should figure out an ending and then start mapping out, like, the stage direction and the dialogue and stuff," Elena began, searching for her calendar in the scattered mess of her bag.

"Yeah, I'm sort of depending on you for the dialogue," he said, as he scrambled to stand. "We all have our strengths, and that one's yours."

She began packing the stack of scribbled papers away in her notebook. She was flattered by Alex's surprising comment that she was better at writing dialogue. Even though she would probably end up with the bulk of the detail work, it didn't bother her. She was proud to be good at something.

They finished packing up and began the descent down the walking path that led back into town. She never would have predicted a boy who slept through class and a girl who dreamed with her eyes open could produce tangible work.

"I think we might actually be able to pull this off," Elena mused aloud as she stumbled on a knot of roots.

"See." He lent her his arm to steady her on the uneven ground. "Told you we'd balance each other out."

To: dramagirl23@email.com
From: LanieH@email.com
Subject: A quick hello

Hi Claire Bear,

Just finished meeting with Alex about our project. He's not such a flake after all. I think I sort of underestimated him. We definitely made progress on our play today. I'm still having

fun with this whole playwriting thing. I don't know if we'll be one of the final plays selected, but we're definitely enjoying ourselves.

How are you? I just realized today that Halloween is in a couple of weeks. Any cool parties? I don't think they really celebrate Halloween here. Well, they have their own version of it. (Actually, I think theirs might be the original Halloween— you know, what our version of Halloween grew out of.) It's called Todos los Santos, or All Saints' Day, here, and they celebrate it on Nov. 1. It doesn't sound quite as fun as Halloween, to be honest. My host family is going to take me to the graveyard to set out flowers for their ancestors. It's to show respect for the dead—a little different than our holiday. The good thing is that we get that Monday off of school and Señora Cruz is making a big dinner. Happy early Halloween!

Love,

Elena

On the Thursday after Halloween Elena and Jenna decided they should make another outing to the tapas bars the next week. Elena told Alex about the plan that afternoon while they worked on their play. She told him to invite Chris. Jenna rounded up Caitlin and Marci to come along, as well. They assembled at the bar where Elena had first spotted Miguel. It was only eight thirty, which was early by Spain standards, so the restaurant wasn't too crowded yet and there was room for everyone to spread out along the tapas-covered bar.

Jenna ordered a round of sangrias and began pulling plates from the edge of the bar.

"How are the plans coming for the Madrid trip next weekend?" Elena asked, sidling up to Jenna and Alex.

"Pretty good. I found a hostel near the Puerta del Sol with beds available. If we all split the cost of everything, it should be pretty cheap."

"We just have to figure out how we're going to get there."

"I was thinking maybe we'd hitchhike."

"Jenna, are you kidding? We're not hitchhiking across Spain." Elena grabbed a plate of *pan con tomate*.

"Why not? I thought we could have, like, an adventure on our way to Madrid."

"Jenna, I think hitchhiking is a little dangerous, don't you?" Elena prodded. "Plus, who's going to pick up six hitchhikers?"

"Well, I guess we'll just have to find some cars then."

Elena looked up at the front door and saw Miguel and Borja entering the restaurant. She nudged Jenna.

Jenna waved them over to the group.

"Hi guys," Jenna said. "Here, I'll get you some sangrias." She leaned into the bar and flagged down the bartender.

"So, what is going on?" Miguel asked.

"Jenna and I were just talking about our plans for next weekend," Elena said.

"We're taking a trip to Madrid." Jenna handed each boy a glass. "Do you guys know where we can rent cars?"

"Why do you need cars to go to Madrid?" Borja looked genuinely puzzled.

"Well, how else should we get there? Elena shot down my hitchhiking idea," Jenna said.

"Trains are the way to travel here." Miguel chuckled. "What is it with Americans and your obsession with cars?"

"Oh my God. I didn't even think of a train. You guys should come with us next weekend! We need you. It'll be so much fun," Jenna pleaded.

Miguel touched his chin and appeared to be thinking it over. "I will see if I can get off work."

"I can go." Borja smiled broadly at Jenna.

"All right," Jenna whooped. "This is going to be awesome."

They hung close as a group until Alex and Chris wandered off to talk to three pretty Spanish girls who had come in, and Marci and Caitlin headed out onto the dance floor. Jenna talked with Borja, but Elena noticed that she kept stealing glances at Alex.

"So, do you think you'll be able to come with us to Madrid?" Elena asked Miguel after he had ordered another glass of sangria from the bartender.

"I think so. I have to check with my manager, but I would like to go. It would be good to visit again before I go there for university next fall."

"That's right," Elena nodded. "You mentioned you'll be

going to school there. What are you planning to study?"

"I don't know." He leaned back against the bar and looked out at the dance floor, which was filling rapidly. "I love history. Or maybe philosophy. What about you? Do you know what you will study at university?"

"Well, first I have to figure out where I want to go." She hedged for a second, and then surprised herself by opening up a little more. "Maybe I'll study theater, or film." She smiled. She'd never said those words aloud to anyone but Claire.

Jenna interrupted them, grabbing Elena and Miguel by the hand and pulling them toward the dance floor. "Enough talk," she shouted over the music. "Time to dance."

They danced for an hour as a big group. No couples split off, though Elena caught Jenna and Alex eyeing each other throughout the night. At the end of the night, Alex and Chris walked Jenna and Elena back to their respective places to make sure they were safe.

They dropped Jenna off at the dorms and then continued toward the Cruzes' apartment.

"Do you want to meet again tomorrow to work on the play?" Alex asked as they passed through a puddle of light from one of the streetlamps.

"We probably should, huh? I feel like we still have so much to do."

"Well, at least we've finished the first act."

"Yeah, but that took a while."

"We'll get there, Elena. Why don't we meet at that park

down by the marina tomorrow. I'll bring food—my host mom makes these killer *bocadillos*."

They reached the front stoop of the apartment building.

"Thanks for walking me home, boys," Elena said. She waved as they turned to leave. She appreciated the gesture, but she realized that she felt very safe in San Sebastián. After only a couple months, she was already surprisingly comfortable. She wasn't really nervous anymore about going to Madrid. It would be a different experience, but she was ready for another frontier to explore.

Chapter Nine

The swift shimmy of the train as it switched across a fork in the tracks jostled Elena from her nap. The week had passed quickly in a blur of schoolwork and trips to the beach before the weather turned cold. By Saturday she found herself on a train streaking toward Madrid.

Elena sat up in the thinly padded seat and craned her neck to see what everyone else was doing. Jenna was asleep beside her. Marci and Caitlin were reading magazines and whispering. She got up out of her seat and headed toward the bathroom, passing the four boys—Miguel, Borja, Alex, and Chris—sitting in seats that faced each other, playing

cards. As Elena passed them, Miguel caught her eye and smiled. She was glad Miguel had been able to come along. Even though just looking at him made her heart race and the blood rush into her face, and even though she could barely bring herself to say more than two words in his presence, she liked having him around.

Elena stopped for a moment beside the wide glass windows that revealed dry shrubbery and hills whipping by on the other side. The sun was going down over the landscape, which meant they were set to arrive in Spain's capital within the hour.

After eight hours on the train, they reached Madrid just after sundown. They climbed off the train and into Madrid's central station, Estación de Atocha. Elena and her friends passed through a corridor and then boarded a human conveyor belt that looked like an escalator, but with a flat floor instead of stairs, that carried them up to the next level. They entered the core of the station, where they were engulfed by noise and a flurry of sights. The station's intercom system snapped and crackled, announcing departure times in rapid Spanish. The train announcement board clicked as it shuffled letters and numbers with updated departure information. This station was a far cry from the modest one-room train station they'd left in San Sebastián.

A woman in four-inch Jimmy Choos hustled past them, a sprinter on stilts, hurrying to meet a train.

"No need for her to hurry," Miguel assured as they turned

138

to watch her skittering across the marble floor. "Her train will probably be late."

"How do you know?"

"The Germans," he said, "their trains are on time. The Spanish don't stress so much. Five minutes here, ten minutes there. What does it matter over a lifetime?"

Their groggy group followed the signs marked SALIDA that led them to the main corridor.

"Okay," Elena said as they huddled under one of the palm fronds that stretched out over the walkway. "Where do we go now?"

Her friends were yapping over one another, and drifting out across the walkway into the foot traffic. She decided it was going to be nearly impossible to keep a group of eight people together for an entire weekend.

Miguel moved toward Elena and held his Madrid pocket map out in front of them. She liked having him so close, though it made her stomach knot up. She tried to relax. *He's just my friend,* she told herself. She tried to think of him the way she thought of Alex, which worked only as long as she didn't look at Miguel and he didn't talk.

"We are here now." He pointed to a dot in the right corner of the map, then traced toward the center with his finger. "And our hostel is here, near the Puerta del Sol. I think we will need to take the metro."

"Metro?" Jenna craned her neck over Elena's shoulder to peer at the map.

"Um, underground train. How do you say it in English?"

"Subway," Elena said. "So, how do we do that?"

"I think we ask someone," he responded.

"Good idea. Why don't you and Borja go ask and I'll watch your bags," Elena suggested.

His face crinkled into a sly smile and he glanced over his shoulder at the desk labeled INFORMACIÓN.

"Why don't you ask over there and I will watch *your* bag?"

"What? You're Spanish; you should go ask." Elena crossed her arms defensively over her chest.

"Yes, but you are a visitor in Spain who would like to speak the language with more than just your Spanish family. It will be good practice."

"Well, what do I say?" she asked.

"All you have to do is ask how to get from here to the Puerta del Sol," he murmured, handing her the map. "You know the language. Just try it." His eyes were soft. He seemed to be trying to apologize for the spontaneous dare. Elena hated dares. She tried to hate Miguel, too.

"Fine." She snatched the little map from his outstretched hand. "I'll go ask, *in Spanish*, how to get to the hostel." What was she really afraid of? She'd tripped up on her first day in Spain. Wasn't it about time to try speaking Spanish with a stranger again?

"Hola," she mumbled as she approached a woman with a pixie haircut and a small pointed nose, whose head and shoulders barely hovered above the information countertop.

140

"¿Cómo puedo ayudarle?" she asked with a welcoming smile. *Okay*, Elena thought, *she just asked how she can help me. I got that.*

"¿Cómo puedo llegar allí desde aquí?" Elena pointed to a dot on the map near the hostel location.

The woman nodded and began rattling off directions. Elena's mind froze, as it always did when people spoke Spanish rapidly. Her brain couldn't translate all the words fast enough, so they just ended up jumbled together inside her head. It would be so embarrassing if she couldn't pull this off. All she had to do was ask directions. Why did she get so nervous making conversation that wasn't outlined in a textbook? She peered back over her shoulder where Jenna and Miguel smiled at her, urging her on.

"Perdón," Elena interrupted. *"¿Habla despacio, por favor?"* The woman smiled again.

"Por supuesto," she said, then began to speak much more slowly, just as Elena had asked. She rounded out each word and kept her eyes trained on Elena's face to make sure she was comprehending. Then something miraculous happened; Elena began to understand.

After the tiny woman had described how to find the metro, which line to take, and where to get off, Elena thanked her effusively. She was so grateful for the woman's kindness and patience that she felt like reaching across the counter, picking her up, and swinging her around the train station. Instead she thanked her and walked back to the

group, where she reported what she'd learned then led the way toward the metro.

As they bumped and jostled their way onto the metro car, Miguel leaned in toward Elena's ear. "I knew you could speak Spanish," Miguel said as he found a place to stand. "Pretty soon you will be speaking better Spanish than me." Miguel smiled.

"I don't think so." She laughed. "Thank you, though." She forced herself to meet his eyes for once. "I mean, thanks for pushing me to try my Spanish." She knew it was Miguel's belief in her ability to speak Spanish that made her try again, however reluctantly. For that, she was grateful.

The metro spit the group out into the buzzing center of Puerta del Sol, Madrid's central plaza. In the center of the plaza sat a large saucer-shaped fountain and a tall statue of a man on horseback. The square was hedged in on all sides by wide buildings painted the pale yellow color of lemon chiffon cake with vanilla frosting trim.

The Puerta del Sol was believed by many to be the heart of the city because it was situated in the city's physical center. In fact, it was the geographical center of the entire country. Elena felt that heart was an appropriate word for the plaza since it virtually pulsed, pumping people and cars through the streets that radiated out from its center like arteries. As the masses of people coursed past her, Elena pulled her backpack to the front of her body. She was in a big city now; she had to be more mindful of herself and her things. She'd been warned by the Cruzes about pickpockets who lingered near the fountain.

After several trips around the block, they managed to hunt down their tiny hostel. Jenna checked them in.

"We're going to do all the big-city stuff while we're here—go to the cool clubs, eat at great restaurants, hear awesome music," Jenna reminded them as they trudged up the stairs to their rooms to get ready for their first night in Madrid. "We're going big, you guys."

Later that evening they met in front of the hostel and walked several blocks to their dinner destination. The flamenco restaurant Borja selected was small, dark, and smelled of stale smoke. It was also packed from the front rim of the stage to the back wall. As it turned out Borja had stumbled on one of the hottest flamenco restaurants in town. They had to wait for an hour, smooshed next to a tiny bar. By the time the hostess had cleared two tables to push together for their large group, Elena's stomach was gurgling at her. But the table, only one row back from the stage, was worth the wait. Elena chose a seat at the far corner, so close to the front of the stage she could see the black scuffs left from dancers' heels on the wood.

Miguel slipped into a seat beside Elena. Jenna gave her a raised-eyebrow look as if to say, *Isn't it interesting that he chose* that *seat, right next to you.* Elena bowed her head and smiled shyly. She had noticed that Miguel stayed near her

lately, but in a friendly way. Elena was starting to pick up on the fact that he might not be head over heels for Jenna, but she still wasn't convinced that he was interested in her.

Miguel and Borja, their resident food experts, ordered an assortment of tapas and entrées for the table to share. Miguel chose several plates of white asparagus, a fish dish— Mediterranean bream char-grilled over hot coals—sirloin steak with red peppers, and stuffed mushrooms. When the waitress delivered the first round of food and two pitchers of sangria, a cloud of spicy, woody scents mingled together over the table. Moments later the house lights dimmed so that the only light in the restaurant came from the white tea lights winking in the center of each table. A flutter of plucked guitar strings unfolded in the darkened room. A clack of castanets bounced off the walls. The guitarist was illuminated first, sitting on a wooden stool off to the side of the stage, his fingers galloping across the strings. A voice tinged with sadness lifted up into the air in a haunting lilt.

A woman's form broke into the light, slinking and twisting. Her tiered dress, in shots of claret and black, swirled around her as though it were dancing independent of her, yet at her will. She rattled the castanets in time to the music and knocked her heels against the hollow stage.

"This music is sexy." Jenna leaned across the table to whisper, then winked at Elena. Elena noticed her lean a little in Alex's direction.

Elena smiled softly then reached across the table toward

the water pitcher and filled her glass. Suddenly the room took a collective breath.

Elena looked up at the stage just in time to see the dancer scampering offstage like a wounded deer. The guitarist kept singing and playing.

"What happened?" she whispered to Miguel.

"It looked like she must have tripped on a groove in the stage and twisted her ankle." He shook his head in disbelief. "I have never seen this happen before."

There was a crackling tension in the air as they waited to see what came next.

"I wonder if this is the end," Elena whispered to Miguel.

As soon as the words left her mouth, a different woman slithered out of the darkness. She felt Miguel shift in his chair, moving closer to her. He leaned in and lingered near her ear for a moment.

"Or it could be just the beginning," he whispered. A ripple of shivers crawled across Elena's skin.

The new dancer was dressed in a brilliant pink dress. Her light brown hair looked hastily slicked into a chignon and pierced with a floppy purple flower. The rushed hairstyle and a brief flush in her cheeks were the only clues that betrayed how quickly she'd had to scramble onstage to cover the mishap. She flipped open a lace fan and twirled it, her wrist flicking and spinning, her legs moving beneath her like liquid. Her motions were so fluid and feminine, yet so sure.

"She is wonderful," Miguel whispered in Elena's ear.

"How is she able to do that, to just step in like that without missing a beat?" Elena asked.

"It is the nature of flamenco," he explained. "It is an art of improvisation. They may practice their performances for this restaurant, but true flamenco musicians are masters at making it up onstage. It is like your American jazz in that way."

"So she's a true flamenco performer?"

He nodded, shifting his eyes back to the dancer as she floated across the stage. Elena wondered if she'd ever possess that kind of confidence.

Two more flamenco dancers gave solo performances. To end the show, all the dancers, except for the one who twisted her ankle, came out and performed together, their bright colored dresses twirling past one another across the stage.

The next morning they had a group discussion about how to spend their day. The original plan had been to see a museum and a bullfight, but they had trouble getting started in the morning. Jenna and Alex both overslept, and it had taken longer than expected for everyone to shower and get dressed. When they had finally assembled in the hostel's dining room for a late breakfast, it had become clear that they were not going to be able to do everything they had planned.

"We could split up," Jenna suggested, grabbing a croissant from a basket. "I mean, I don't really want to, but at least that way everyone could see what they want to see before we leave."

"Well, I'd prefer to go to the museums," Elena said. Caitlin and Marci agreed.

"My vote is for the bullfight, man," Alex chimed in.

"Me, too," Jenna seconded.

Chris and Borja agreed that they wanted to see the bull-fight, but Miguel was the only boy who hedged.

"I've seen plenty of bullfights," he explained.

"Cool. You can come to the museum with us," Elena said casually, though inside she was elated.

The two groups headed their separate ways and planned to meet up at the train station later in the evening.

Elena and her group took the metro and exited the sta-tion at the park-lined Paseo del Prado, one of the widest and busiest streets in Madrid. Elena was surprised by how green it was. Trees lined the wide promenade leading toward the three world-famous art museums. Elena breathed in the fresh air. She could feel autumn in this inland city more so than in San Sebastián, where the air was heavy with salt water.

They approached the Prado Museum, arguably the most famous in Madrid. It reminded Elena of a slicker version of an ancient Greek temple with smooth stone columns, topped by an intricately carved mural. She felt this was a good indication of the grandeur and history that lay inside.

Only minutes after entering the museum, Elena was struck by how many different types of paintings from all over Europe were housed under one roof. There was a blurb at

the bottom of a brochure stating that the Prado owned over nine thousand works of art in total. Not all of them were on display, of course, but it certainly seemed that way to Elena.

"Oh my God," she murmured. "I don't think we could see everything even if we had the whole week."

"I know." Marci groaned.

"We don't have to see it all," Miguel pointed out. "Perhaps we should just focus on the Spanish art. That alone may take all afternoon." He pointed out an entire floor on the map reserved for the Spanish masters.

They meandered past centuries of Dutch and German art, through corridors of Italy's finest, and finally found their way to the floor reserved for the Spanish masters.

"What are we supposed to be looking for?" Caitlin whispered.

Elena shrugged. "Just absorb them, I guess."

"What makes these so good anyway?" Caitlin asked. Marci steered them toward a Velásquez painting just as a guided tour led in Spanish filed away from it.

"Take this one. I think I've seen it before." Caitlin tilted her head and scrunched her nose.

Elena nodded. She recognized it as the painting on the cover of her Spanish textbook.

"But why is it famous?" Caitlin said.

Miguel read the Spanish blurb aloud about LA INFANTA MARGARITA, and then gave them a recap in English. When he was done, the girls leaned in closer.

"I still don't get it," Caitlin whispered to Marci in a tone that was loud enough for Elena to overhear. "This is kind of boring."

Marci rolled her eyes and took Caitlin by the arm, leading her toward the next painting along the wall. Elena hung back so she could consider the first painting without Caitlin's interruptions. Miguel didn't make a move to follow Marci and Caitlin either.

"What do you think?" he asked after a long moment of silence had passed while they contemplated the painting.

"I don't know. I'm not really an art buff, or anything, but I think it's pretty. What about this one?" she asked, moving to a portrait of a woman several paces down the wall. "What do you think of her?"

"This woman is beautiful, no?"

Elena nodded emphatically and leaned in to look at the delicate brushstrokes around her eyes.

"But..." Miguel paused dramatically.

"But what?" she asked, straightening up to look at him.

"Well, I would like her better if her eyes were blue." He looked forward, appearing to study the painting closely. "And if her hair was lighter. If her skin was very fair, and if she had lips like..." He looked at Elena boldly. She froze and looked right back. "Yes. If she had lips like yours, then I would think she was even more beautiful." He smiled slightly.

Elena reflexively reached up to touch her lips and felt a blush rising in her cheeks. *He's flirting with me*, she thought.

For a moment she felt time freeze. She imagined herself laugh and smile then say something flirty in return as she bumped playfully into him. But she realized none of that was happening. Miguel looked at her expectantly.

She tried to say the things that were in her head, but what she heard come out of her mouth was, "We should probably catch up with Marci and Caitlin." She smiled weakly and peered down the corridor in the girls' direction.

Elena and Miguel fell in step with Marci and Caitlin at the end of the Velásquez display, and they all wandered toward the section on Francisco de Goya.

"I'm going to like these," Caitlin predicted. "Goya, Goya, Goya. Even the name is fun to say."

They edged in next to a cluster of tourists assembled in front of a painting of a nude woman reclining on a settee, her arms folded confidently behind her head.

Miguel read the blurb in Spanish again. Elena stepped closer to the painting, listening to the musical rise and fall of Miguel's voice, but tuning out the actual words. The best part about seeing these paintings in person was being able to move close enough to see the texture of the brushstrokes in the paint. She wanted to reach out and run her fingers over the ripples of paint. These paintings granted immortality to their creators. She felt an urge to create something lasting of her own through playwriting.

"This particular painting by Goya created a new nudity form," Miguel began to translate in a serious academic voice. "It was inspired by Goya's mistress, a lazy woman who enjoyed lying around all day near the window. ..."

Elena straightened up and glanced toward the plaque next to the painting. "Does it really say that?" she gasped.

"Yes," Miguel deadpanned. "It also says that Goya wanted her to go on a diet, but she refused to give up *churros con chocolate*." He flashed a sly smile.

Elena burst into giggles.

"Mmm, *churros con chocolate*," Caitlin groaned deliriously.

"Speaking of food, we might want to leave soon so we can grab something to eat before our train," Marci said.

"Good idea, I'm starving," Caitlin said, hooking her arm through Marci's and leading the way to the exit.

"Hey, you guys." Jenna waved as Elena's group walked toward the platform that boarded the train headed back to San Sebastián.

"How was the bullfight?" Elena asked as they approached the other half of their group.

"It was awesome," Alex gushed.

"What was it like?" Marci leaned in.

"Pretty gross," Jenna admitted, contorting her face in disgust. "And actually sort of boring."

"What? No, it was brilliant," Chris defended.

"The bull was huge," Alex chimed in.

"It was interesting from, like, a historical perspective, but totally macho," Jenna said.

"You have to admit, the bulls looked pretty awesome," Alex countered. "Each one looked like it could break every bone in my body."

"That's impressive?" Jenna shot back with a wry smile, obviously enjoying the heated exchange. "They were just big simple animals."

"Just big simple animals? Are you crazy?" Alex said. "It was sick, dude. The bull charged out like this." He scuffed his foot on the floor and bounded toward Chris. Chris grabbed him around the waist and tried to fling him to the ground, but Alex resisted.

"But the matador was too quick," Chris took over the narration. "He spun around and stabbed the bull in the shoulder." Chris popped Alex on the shoulder with his fist. The boys abandoned their narration but continued to wrestle as other passengers began to board the train.

Jenna picked up her backpack and cracked a smile at the other girls. "Like I said, just big simple animals."

"Hey, what did you call me?" Alex said. He charged over to Jenna, who was already giggling, picked her up by the waist, and carried her onto the train.

Just as Elena was beginning to feel a twinge of snack-sized hunger she heard the metallic squeak of the food cart wheels bumping down the aisle. She and Alex had left the others and had come to another car to work on their play assignment, which was due in only a few days. Elena knew they had a lot of work to do, but her mind kept drifting back to Miguel's flirtations back at the museum. It was so much better than anything she could have dreamed up.

There was a whooshing sound and the compartment dimmed as the train sped through a tunnel and the view of twilight outside her window turned completely black. Elena was grateful for the few moments of darkness to think about Miguel. By the time they had exited the tunnel, the snack attendant was standing beside her.

"Something to eat?" the attendant asked.

"Yes," she answered, pointing to a package of chocolate hazelnut cookies. She was always amazed when many of the locals instantly knew she was an English speaker. She knew she didn't look particularly Spanish, but there seemed to be something about her appearance that screamed "American."

"And a water," she said.

"With gas?" he asked as he handed her the cookies.

She shook her head no. Elena had learned her lesson with that question. She'd finally realized that the servers weren't asking her if she wanted a glass. They were actually saying gas, and gas referred to the bubbles added to the water.

Elena split the paper wrapping on the package of cookies and spread them out on a napkin.

"Help, I can't eat all of these," she said, shoving the cookies into the middle of the table that stood between them. It was funny how much Alex had begun to feel like one of her

brothers. Elena had noticed that being with people who were all so far from home was like being in a friendship incubator, accelerating the awkward phase and skipping more quickly into the comfortable stage.

"Okay, we should probably work on the third act. That's the only thing we still need to finish," Elena said, pulling her notebook out of her backpack and spreading it open on top of the table. Elena wrote *Act Three* at the top of the page.

"Right," Alex nodded, reaching for a cookie. "So, he's already met his mom. We just need to wrap up the love story. I think they should end up together, and maybe they kiss at the end."

"I don't know," Elena said after a pause.

"What? You don't like it?"

Elena hesitated again. "It's not that. I just don't know if it's very realistic."

"Elena. What are you talking about? We've been building up to it the entire play."

"It's just that sometimes two people have trouble getting together, and it may never happen, whatever the reason."

"What?" He looked at her sideways for a moment, then said, "Ooh, is this about you and Miguel?"

"What are you talking about?"

"You know what I mean. I saw him following you around all weekend, and I saw you looking at him, too."

"What?"

"He's into you, you know."

154

She was used to guys falling all over themselves to be near Gwen, and now Jenna. So, even after Miguel's constant proximity and his flirtatious comments at the museum, Elena had trouble believing he was interested in her.

"Do you really think Miguel likes me?" she asked.

"Yeah, why not?"

"I don't know. I had just assumed he was into Jenna."

"Yeah," he sighed. "She *is* hot."

"That's what I mean. Everyone loves her."

"Look, Elena, Jenna's a cute girl, but that doesn't mean you're not."

"Aw, that's a nice compliment. You know, in an Alex sort of way." She laughed.

He tugged at the side of his baseball cap. "I just mean that you're a good-looking girl. Maybe Jenna's not his type. It is actually possible, you know."

Elena wondered if she had spent so many years comparing herself to her sister's impossible beauty that she hadn't really looked at herself the way Miguel might.

"Listen, I don't know what Miguel's done to let you know he's interested, but you can't expect him to do *all* the work. Most guys are okay with making a move, but they need some sort of sign that you're interested, too. They need to know they aren't going to get shot down. No one likes to be rejected."

Elena thought about Miguel's flirtatious comments again and tried to remember how she'd responded. She had

imagined the perfect response, but she hadn't really done anything to reciprocate.

Alex leaned in a little closer and softened his tone. "I'm just reaching here, but my guess is you probably haven't done much to let him know you like him."

"How do *you* even know I like him?" she recoiled, her face burning.

"Oh, please. It's so obvious."

"Well if it's so obvious—"

"To me, not to Miguel," he countered, before she could even get her argument out.

"All right, I get it," she said. "So, to recap, I'm irresistible, Miguel's irresistible, we're all irresistible." She cut her eyes at him and then blinked furiously in her best playful Jenna impression.

Alex laughed.

"Enough about me." She scooted the notebook and pen over toward Alex. "We have a play to finish." She was trying to appear as though she had brushed the whole conversation aside easily, but she knew this would stay with her. Alex had just challenged everything she had ever believed about herself and her prospects with boys. He had actually suggested that someone could like her just for being herself.

Chapter Ten

"What do you think? Should we change it?" Elena asked as she and Alex were walking toward play production on Wednesday. They were supposed to turn in their play at the beginning of class. "We still have a few minutes."

"Elena, would you stop stressing?" Alex leaned against the outside wall of the classroom.

"I just feel like we could have done something more with the confrontation with the mother, and—"

"Elena, it's perfect." Alex snatched the play out of her hand and walked into the classroom. She was about to make

one last protest when she saw him slide the stack of papers into Ms. B's hands.

"Thank you, Alex," Ms. B said as she set their play on top of the others on her desk. Then she looked at Elena. "I'm looking forward to reading it."

Elena nodded weakly, then took her seat.

"Stop worrying," Alex whispered as he sat down in the desk beside her. "It's done now. All we can do is wait."

Despite Alex's insistence that worrying wasn't going to change anything, Elena had reviewed their play over and over in her head all day. That night at the apartment she decided she would call her great-aunt Elena to see if she could visit her in Barcelona over the next weekend. She'd realized a couple days earlier that next week would be Thanksgiving. She and her friends were planning to make a little outing to the tapas bars to celebrate, but Elena also felt like being with family, even if it was family she'd never met. Besides, she figured if she was busy traveling and meeting new people, she wouldn't be able to spend the entire week-end worrying over Ms. B's decision.

She dug through her bag and found the slip of paper with her great-aunt's phone number. Her mom had also written her calling card number to use so the Cruzes wouldn't be charged for her calls.

She walked into the empty kitchen and dialed the phone. A recorded voice picked up after three rings. Elena left a message in the best Spanish she could muster. She knew it was sort of rude to call up and ask to come and stay for the weekend with only a week's notice, but she hoped her great-aunt wouldn't mind. With the anxiety over the play, and the sadness of spending Thanksgiving without her family, she knew a trip to Barcelona would be a welcome distraction.

Late the following Saturday afternoon Elena found herself walking through Barcelona. Her great-aunt had called her back right away to say she was more than welcome to come for a visit. Great-Aunt Elena had offered to meet her at the train, but Elena didn't want to cause her any trouble. And to her surprise, she was actually a bit excited about the thought of exploring Barcelona—if only a little bit—on her own.

As soon as she stepped out of the train station, it became clear that although Barcelona was a beach town, like San Sebastián, it was also a big city. The air was filled with the smell of the ocean and the sounds of people and traffic. On her way to her great-aunt's place she strolled up la Rambla, which served as town square, shopping mall, meeting place, and people-watchers' paradise. As she walked alone up the street, which was blocked from all cars, she passed a raggedy group of jugglers, a fortune-teller, and a tight-faced woman dressed in head-to-toe Prada. It was a carnival of sight and sound. Miguel had told her that people gathered at la Rambla during all hours. If you wandered through at two in the morning, there would be people hanging out,

playing the guitar, kissing on the corners, living life.

As Elena ventured off la Rambla and wound through a jumble of intersecting streets, walking toward her great-aunt Elena's condo, she reflected on how independent she had become, traveling alone in a foreign country.

Finally Elena came upon her great-aunt's condo. It was the only stoop among its drab white counterparts with a door painted turquoise and framed with hanging flowering plants. Wire baskets overflowed with bougainvillea, and potted plants lined the steps. Elena had only heard a few things about her great-aunt Elena, but from the little she did know, she wasn't surprised that the woman had the most colorful home on the block.

She'd barely knocked when the door opened and Elena found herself staring at two women who looked exactly like each other and vaguely like her own mother. Her mother's features were there, but the noses were slightly larger, the eyes a shade lighter, the hair a bit curlier.

"Hola," the two women cheered. *"Somos primas de tu madre."* Of course. They were her mom's cousins. Twins named Anna and Paloma Delgado. *"Bienvenido,"* the twins echoed each other as they motioned for Elena to come into the foyer. As soon as Elena stepped over the threshold, the sweet smell of flowers was replaced with the scent of cooking. The aroma of spices, sangria, and roasting ham permeated the air. The smells made Elena feel instantly at home.

The twins ushered Elena into the living room, a warm

space made warmer by the people gathered inside. They rose together and sang out to her like a chorus, their *"holas"* and *"bienvenidos"* veering together in harmony. The previous night on the phone her great-aunt Elena had warned her that she'd invited a few relatives over for dinner. Elena was picturing a small gathering, enough maybe for three-on-three basketball. But this was an entire football squad.

As Elena entered the room she was buried under an avalanche of hugs and cheek kisses. The twins proceeded to introduce her to more people than she could possibly remember. She was surprised by how many traces of her own immediate family she spotted before her. It was as though her mother and siblings were potato-head dolls whose features had been yanked off and spread around the room. Cousins Paloma and Anna had her mom's Popsicle-stick legs. Tio Mateo had the same nose as Caleb, with a bump along the bridge, and Tia Alberta had Gwen's black hair. Then there were the ones who didn't look like anyone else. Elena counted herself among that group.

As she neared the end of the introductions, the crowd of people parted to reveal an elderly woman dressed in a pressed green wool pantsuit and matching hat. There was something in the way she held herself that said, *I may look old to you, but I'm as young as I want to be.*

"Elena, es un placer para mi que presentarle tu tia Elena," Paloma introduced the two Elenas.

The elder Elena swept the younger into a hug.

"Welcome, Elena," her great-aunt said in impeccably clear English, then held Elena out at arm's length to get a look at her. "We are so happy you could come visit us."

Great-Aunt Elena had Gwen's eyes; or, rather, Gwen had inherited Great-Aunt Elena's eyes, dipped down slightly at the corners. Gwen often complained that people assumed she was upset when she wasn't smiling. However, on Great-Aunt Elena they were understanding eyes. Without her saying a word, Elena knew that her great-aunt was the kind of person she would tell all her secrets to in one night.

Sometime during her stirring welcome, Elena's bag had been whisked from her hands and set at the foot of the stairs. She was shown to a stuffed chair in the middle of the room, and someone had set a fizzing Orange Fanta in a slender glass on a table beside her chair.

It was a cozy room full of soft places to sit. There was a plump rose-colored sofa, big puffy armchairs, and ottomans. The layout of the place was open, with the dining room, kitchen, and back patio flowing one into the next. "Perfect for entertaining," she could practically hear her mother cooing to a client. However, this wasn't one of the boxy beige houses her mother often showed. In this house, yards and yards of paint-layered canvas covered the walls. She wondered if any of the art—painted in a range of styles—was the work of her great-aunt. The paintings hung side by side, running across the walls in a checkerboard of color. They were depictions of Spanish sunsets and architecture, the beach at dawn, church steeples, children flashing wide messy grins, old men, glittering lakes. Some of them were beautiful and some startling, but all of them were full of emotion. Elena wanted to paint herself into the corner of one and disappear into it for a while. She smiled at the thought, then realized someone was asking her a question in Spanish. She concentrated on the question.

"What do you think of Spain?" a man named Diego repeated. He had been introduced as Elena's second cousin, or perhaps he was someone's husband. There were so many of them, it was hard to remember all their names and the complicated ways they were all related to her.

"I love it here," she answered cautiously, testing the words out in her mind before she let them leave her mouth. "There are so many things I still want to do and see, but I have less than a month left here."

The faces around the room nodded sympathetically, as if they could think of nothing worse than being ripped from Spain before you were ready to leave.

"You don't look particularly Spanish," a woman in red observed timidly.

"Well, my dad's ancestors are English and Swedish. I take after him." It was the same answer she'd given to the countless inquiries over the years about why she didn't look like her siblings. She'd done a lot of explaining since coming to Spain due to her incongruous Spanish first name.

Elena could feel more questions coming.

"Do you prefer our *fútbol* or American football?"

"I'm not that into sports. But I love how proud Spanish people are about their soccer, I mean *fútbol* teams."

"What are your hobbies?"

"What do American girls do for fun?"

"Do you like school?"

"What are you studying?"

"How is America different from Spain?"

So many questions and they were all directed at her. For the first time Elena was the axis of a room. It was thrilling and embarrassing at the same time. This was one of the things she had fantasized about before she'd come to San Sebastián. She wanted to stand out, to be the interesting one in the room. Until now, she'd never realized how much she counted on Gwen to absorb the attention, and Caleb and Jeremy to keep everyone entertained. Being the center of attention was a heavy burden for someone who spent so much time living in her own head.

"Bueno, bueno," Great-Aunt Elena interjected after listening for most of the interview. "We should let our guest rest after her long trip. Come, Elena, I will show you where you will sleep tonight." The chorus of relatives let out a disappointed sigh. "Don't worry. You will all have a chance to ask your questions at dinner."

Aunt Elena led her to the stairs, where she tested the weight of Elena's overnight bag. *"Tómelo,"* she said, handing the bag off to Elena. "Years ago I would have carried it for you, but I'm not as strong as I was once." She flexed a non-existent bicep muscle as evidence and chuckled. "Come, follow an old, frail woman up the stairs." Elena trudged behind her with the bag slung over her shoulder as Great-Aunt Elena moved briskly up the stairs. She might have been an old woman, and perhaps her body wasn't as strong as it once was, but there was certainly nothing frail about her.

The elder Elena led the way through the first door across the top landing.

"This is where you will stay tonight," she announced, showing Elena into the little room. Aunt Elena yanked on a handle at the top of a tall wooden plank along the wall. It lowered to reveal a mattress that settled on the ground like a normal bed. "You'll be sleeping with the lovely ladies." She made a sweeping gesture toward one wall with built-in shelves housing rows and rows of hats.

"These are beautiful." Elena reached her fingers toward a gray felt hat and touched the silky feathers that lay across the brim like a protective wing.

"I'm glad you like them." Great-Aunt Elena beamed. "This one took me a month because I couldn't find the right feathers. What do you think?" She placed the hat on Elena's head and turned her toward the antique mirror suspended on the opposite wall.

"Wait, you made this?" Elena gasped, as she tipped her

chin up a bit to get a better view of herself in the hat.

"I made all of them." Great-Aunt Elena laughed. "It's what I do."

Elena turned toward her great-aunt to ponder the woman in a new light.

"I'm an artist," Great-Aunt Elena continued. "I've been painting for decades. The hats are my latest outlet."

"My brother Jeremy told me you were an artist. Are any of these paintings yours?" Elena asked, gesturing toward the paintings on the far wall.

"*Sí,*" the elder Elena nodded. "All of them."

"All of them? Even the ones downstairs?" she asked as she approached a framed painting that looked different from the others, with murky swirls of paint that seemed to vaguely represent something, though she couldn't tell what.

"This one is a painting of a dream I had."

"You paint your dreams?"

"Well, I've only painted a few actual dreams, but all my paintings represent dreams in a way. Dreams for the future; dreams of what could be or should be. I've always been considered something of a dreamer," Great-Aunt Elena whispered conspiratorially.

"Me, too," Elena divulged. "I mean, my family is always telling me I have my head in the clouds."

"Well, where else would you want your head to be, stuck in the ground?" The older woman laughed heartily.

Elena nodded. "I guess some people just think it's better

to be realistic. You know, to see things the way they really are. My family thinks that all the time I spend daydreaming is time I could be using to do something productive."

Great-Aunt Elena fixed those empathetic eyes on her, and Elena knew she understood. "The dreamers like you and I are the ones who see the potential in everything and everyone. That's what dreaming really is, imagining what could be. Dreaming isn't wasted time. The waste comes when you have these wonderful dreams, but you don't do anything to make them real."

Elena thought of Miguel, and how she really wanted something to happen with him, something real. Ever since her conversation with Alex on the train, she'd been thinking about the fact that she would have to take some kind of action to show him she was interested. She would have to do something soon. She was running out of time in Spain.

For Elena's welcome dinner her great-aunt had invited a "couple of friends" to join the family. This time Elena was prepared. A couple of friends turned into practically the entire neighborhood. Elena's intimate dinner with family had become a full-blown party with music, drinks, and trays of olives and cheeses set out on tables.

Elena welcomed the party atmosphere. With so many family members crowded into one room, she was beginning to feel as if she hadn't really missed Thanksgiving after all.

"So, you are this American I've been hearing so much about," a stoop-shouldered man with large ears and dark,

sparkly eyes said as he gently pinched Elena's shoulder, perhaps to see if Americans were made of real flesh and blood. "Another beautiful Elena."

Elena giggled nervously. "Well, you're right about my being the American," Elena answered, wondering if this was another relative she hadn't met. "And you are?"

"Allow me to introduce myself; I am Enrique del Toro." He presented himself with a flourish, as though he were announcing a bullfighter entering the ring.

"Nice to meet you," she said, holding back a giggle. This guy was a trip. "How do you know my great-aunt Elena?"

"She is my cousin." They both looked toward the elder Elena, who stood laughing under an arched doorway, the yellow light swimming at her back. "So, do you feel like a Spaniard yet?" he asked.

"I don't know if I will ever feel like a Spaniard."

"But you are part Spanish."

"Yes, but you wouldn't know by looking at me."

"Oh," he waved off her remark. "I have plenty of Spanish friends with light hair, light skin. Being Spanish comes from here." He pointed to his chest.

Elena glanced down at her bare arms folded across her chest. She had expected somehow that coming to Spain might make her more Spanish, that the sun might stain her a shade of brown she'd never been before. But even after nearly three months in Spain, her skin had stubbornly remained the color of skim milk. She wondered why that mattered so much to her. Why did she have to look Spanish in order to feel Spanish? She felt connected to her great-aunt, but not because they looked anything alike. Rather, Elena had the same spirit, the same love of art, and the same romantic outlook. Gwen might have inherited their great-aunt's eyes, but Elena had inherited her belief that the world did not just consist of things she could see and touch.

Great-Aunt Elena clinked a fork against her glass.

"Dinner," she called. "Everyone into the dining room, *por favor.*"

The group piled into the cramped dining room around two tables. After some gentle cajoling, Elena took a seat at the head of the largest table on one side, and Great-Aunt Elena sat across the long wooden plane from her. They were Elena bookends.

Dinner was spread out in mismatched pots and platters like a potluck. There was a kettle of potato soup, several salads, cured ham, and a dish called *ajo de la mano*, which Enrique explained was made of potatoes and chilies and then dressed with garlic and spices, oil and vinegar.

Hours later, over fruit tarts, Elena's family members began to tell stories. Elena was glad to settle back in her chair, full and sleepy from the food and wine.

"Elena," Great-Uncle Roberto, the elder Elena's brother, leaned back in his chair when he addressed her. "Did you know that your namesake is famous in Barcelona for more than just her art? Her parties were legendary."

Great-Aunt Elena laughed and tossed a napkin that landed on Roberto's head, shading his eyes like one of her hats.

"Don't start inventing stories, Roberto."

"It's the truth. You think this gathering is big. You should have seen the parties Elena used to throw here."

Aunt Elena laughed and covered her face with her hands, but she didn't look at all embarrassed. She looked as though she wanted him to continue more than anything.

Roberto proceeded to tell a story about the time his sister had had a three-day-long bash after Barcelona's team won a particularly competitive *fútbol* match. It sounded like something out of *The Great Gatsby*, with people dressed in their finest, drinking and dancing for days on end.

"Your mother was here during that party," Great-Aunt Elena recalled suddenly. "What a fun time."

The fabled stories about the older woman's parties led to talk of past boyfriends.

"There was the one from Holland. He was a pilot," Great-Aunt Elena recalled fondly. "But my favorite was Xavier from Paris," she reminisced. "He was in Barcelona for only three months. We met one night on la Rambla, and we walked and talked until the sun came up. Three months later he was set to move back to Paris. I'd always wanted to go to Paris, perhaps even live there for a while...."

"What happened?" Elena leaned over the table ledge.

"He asked me to marry him."

"What did you say?"

170

"Oh, what could I say? I said no, of course." She laughed. Elena was aghast.

"What about Paris?"

"We went to Paris. I just wasn't ready to get married."

"Elena, your great-aunt has always been good about making things happen the way she would like, and not waiting around for other people to make decisions for her," Roberto added.

Great-Aunt Elena laughed. "You make me sound much too noble, Roberto. Who wants more wine?"

Elena lifted herself up out of her seat and grasped the wine bottle in the middle of the table.

Roberto laughed. "I think you should skip the wine and go to bed."

Elena shook her head, but she knew he was right. She was so tired her eyes could barely stay open. It had been a long day of traveling and meeting new people. Now it was almost three in the morning. She reluctantly said good night to the twenty or so guests who lingered around the table, still talking and picking at the food.

She trudged upstairs and closed the door to her borrowed room, although the hum of chatter seeped through the gap between the door and the carpet. When Elena settled into bed that night, she had a belly plump with food, a head swimming in wine, and a heart full of her namesake's passion for life and love.

• • •

The next morning Elena's great-aunt offered to drive her to the train station. But the older woman insisted that she take Elena on a quick sightseeing trip before she caught her train.

"There is one more thing you have to see before you leave Barcelona," her great-aunt remarked as she turned the little car around the corner and several tall breathtaking spires came into view above the other buildings. "There it is. La Sagrada Família."

The elder Elena parked the car and they stepped out onto the sidewalk.

"Is it a church?" Elena asked. She looked up to take in the massive intricately carved and oddly shaped structure.

"It is a church and a work of art."

It was like something out of a Tim Burton movie—strange, beautiful, and utterly compelling. Elena took her camera out and snapped a few pictures before her great-aunt hurried her back into the car.

"I want to make sure you have plenty of time at the train station," she explained as they pulled away from the curb. Elena turned in her seat to steal one last glance at the towering marvel. It's obscenely high spires were visible even after the rest became obstructed. Elena thought it was the perfect last-glimpse of her time in Barcelona.

They arrived at the station a little early. Since she had some time to kill, Elena hunted down an Internet café and started writing an e-mail to her mom.

To: CarlaHolloway@email.com
From: LanieH@email.com
Subject: Barcelona

Mom, I just left Great-Aunt Elena's house this morning. I'm about to board a train back to San Sebastián, but I found a little Internet café at the train station so I wanted to write you a quick e-mail to let you know how wonderful it was. I loved Great-Aunt Elena, and I'm so proud to be named after her. I think you knew exactly what I would think of her when you insisted I go. I feel like I'm really finding my place, Mom, through my connection with Great-Aunt Elena, and through this playwriting program I'm doing. Thanks for pushing me to make the trip to Barcelona. It was so worth it!

I missed you guys over Thanksgiving, but it was good to be with family this weekend. Luckily, I'll be coming home the week before Christmas, so I won't have to spend two major holidays without you all.

My teacher is announcing the winners of this playwriting contest tomorrow. I am so nervous because I really want the play I wrote with my friend Alex to be chosen. Think good thoughts for me.

Love,

Elena

Chapter Eleven

"This is a disaster," Alex hollered, hurtling his hat through the air. *Nice touch*, Elena thought. They were working through one of Ms. B's improvisation workshops in the theater at school. She was still getting the hang of this improv thing, but Alex had taken to it immediately.

"Just calm down. Take a seat and relax," Elena said in her most even tone.

"How can I calm down?" he bellowed, stomping in circles around the stage. His footsteps were so heavy she could practically see their impressions on the wood like footprints in sand. The last few playwriting classes had taken place in the theater where Ms. B led them through the basics of acting and set design. Elena resisted at first, but Ms. B insisted that in order to be an empathetic director, everyone had to try their hand at acting. The first few times Elena stepped out onto the stage her heart was thudding like a hammer and she couldn't forget all her classmates' eyes that were focused on her. But gradually she'd become less self-conscious. She wasn't exactly comfortable, but she could do it.

This particular day, Ms. B had given Elena and Alex a scene to improvise in which Alex was freaking out, while Elena calmed him down. Elena really felt herself acting. On the surface, she was cool as an iceberg, while inside she was a swirl of anxiety and nerves. Ms. B was set to announce the final plays at the end of class, and Elena could barely contain her restlessness. Finally, Ms. B signaled the end of their scene.

"Thank you, Alex and Elena. Great job." Ms. B joined them in the middle of the stage and made them take a bow. "Always take a bow. You earned it.

"Next class we'll go over sense memory," Ms. B continued as she took a seat on the stage, letting her silk-slippered feet dangle off the side.

Ms. B cleared her throat and pulled her clipboard onto her lap. This was it, Elena thought. She was going to announce the finalists. She could barely sit still. She glanced at Alex, who wasn't even disguising the fact that his eyes

were closed and his head was resting on the back of the seat. Was he seriously going to sleep through this?

"I just want to say you all had particularly strong final plays this year," Ms. B began. "It was difficult for me to choose only two plays because there was so much passion and creativity in all of your writing. You should all be proud."

Elena believed her competition was stiff. But she also suspected some of this speech was meant as a consolation for the losers. She really hoped she wasn't one of them. Not only had she become excited about this for herself, she also didn't want to disappoint Alex, or Ms. B.

"I wish we could stage all your plays, but as you know, we don't have the time or resources to do that."

Elena shifted in her seat again. *Just get to the names,* she thought.

"And I want to praise you for collectively being bold and brave enough to tackle some of the tough teen issues," Ms. B continued. "Like drug abuse, date rape, eating disorders."

Elena silently cursed herself for listening to Alex's idea to set themselves apart by not delving into those very issues. She knew Ms. B would love the drug-overdose idea. It was dark and edgy, but it also had a lesson. Elena was suddenly convinced that Dylan had chosen that topic for her play.

"Okay, so here are the finalists. If I read your name, please stay after class so we can start working out the details. The first play is by Gabe and Dylan, called *The Edge of Sanity.* And the second play is by..."

Elena concentrated on a loose thread at the hem of her jeans.

"…Alex and Elena, called *The Long Journey Home.*"

Elena looked up to see Ms. B staring directly at her and smiling. Elena felt herself smile back, a big smile that bubbled up from inside. She felt herself register victory. It was a strange, unfamiliar sensation that tingled down to her toes.

Alex sat up in his seat, straight as a flagpole.

"We got it!" He threw his arm around Elena's shoulder. Then he lowered his voice and pressed his forehead to Elena's. "We rock, man." She nodded through giddy laughter.

She barely noticed as the rest of the class filed out of the theater and into the cool afternoon. She was in a happiness coma that she knew would last the rest of the day.

Ms. B called the four winners up to the front of the stage and handed out some worksheets outlining a suggested timeline for planning and rehearsing.

"You are going to be responsible for casting your plays, so I suggest you start working on that right away," Ms. B said in a voice that was all business. "You can cast people from this class if you like, but you aren't required to. As we get a little further along we'll talk about set design and props. You'll be responsible for letting me know what you need in terms of props, and I'll assemble a team for each of you to help design the sets and the costumes. My advice is to keep all of these things pretty simple, though. Any questions?"

Elena felt as if she had about a million, but she couldn't

decide which to ask so she shook her head along with the other three.

"Okay, congratulations, you guys." Ms. B hopped down from the stage and began packing up her lesson plans. "Good luck finding great actors."

Elena and Alex walked out under a cloudy sky.

"When do you want to start casting actors?" Elena asked.

"Let's meet tomorrow at the theater to talk about it. I think we should have all the parts filled by this weekend."

Elena agreed, then said good-bye to Alex and started toward the multimedia center to check her e-mail before heading home. She was so excited about their play being chosen, but she was also already worrying about casting. It was obvious that Alex wanted to play the leading man. And most of the other roles were relatively minor, so she didn't think they would be a problem. The only part that could pose a problem was the female lead. Elena knew everyone was probably assuming she would take that part, but she didn't want to appear onstage at all.

The multimedia center was empty, as she'd expected. She logged on and began writing an e-mail to Claire and her mom about the great news.

To: dramagirl23@email.com; CarlaHolloway@email.com
From: LanieH@email.com
Subject: We got it!

Mom and Claire,

I wanted to let you know that my play was chosen as a finalist in the big competition. Now Alex and I have to work on producing this thing. It's going to be a lot of work, but I'm so ready! I'm deliriously happy.

I love you both.

Elena

Elena signed off the computer, grabbed her backpack, and walked back out onto the nearly empty campus. She was walking briskly toward the road when she felt a long set of legs fall into stride with her own.

She looked up and saw that it was Miguel.

"*Hola,* Elena," he said.

"*Hola,* Miguel." She smiled. *"¿Cómo estás?"*

He smiled back and told her in Spanish that he was fine. Elena hadn't slipped immediately into English as she normally did, so he continued in Spanish. "I was just talking with my teacher. We have a big test next week, and I need to do well."

Elena nodded and smiled.

"How are you?" he asked. "You look particularly happy today."

Elena suddenly noticed the broad smile plastered to her face. "Well, actually the play I wrote with Alex for our play production class was chosen as one of the two winners. That means we'll get to stage the play for the school and anyone

else who wants to come in, like, two and a half weeks."

"Wow, that's great."

"It's kind of an honor."

"I'm sure it is. I'm so happy for you, Elena." By the way he opened his eyes wide she could tell he was impressed.

"Thanks. It's something I really wanted, so that's probably why I look so happy."

They approached the edge of campus, where the grass met the sidewalk.

"I have to go to work," Miguel said, jutting his thumb in the direction of the Maria Cristina.

"Okay." She headed in the other direction, toward the Cruzes' apartment. "I'll see you later."

"Elena," he called after she had walked several paces. "Congratulations." Then he winked at her, which was sort of a cheesy thing to do, but it made her light up anyway. She walked out toward the beach and realized that during her whole conversation with Miguel she'd forgotten to be nervous. She hadn't analyzed the way he was talking to her, or the content of what he said. She'd just had a nice, relaxed conversation with him. Plus, she realized that he was the first live person she'd shared her good news with. She almost felt like keeping her news to herself for the rest of the night, so that for a day she and Miguel would be sharing a secret.

Chapter Twelve

By the weekend, Elena and Alex had filled every role in their play except the female lead. To Elena's relief, Alex didn't pressure her into playing the part herself.

"It's cool, Elena," he'd said when she'd defensively listed all the reasons she wasn't prepared to go onstage. "We'll work it out. Just chill."

On Sunday afternoon, their self-imposed deadline for filling all the roles, Elena and Alex sat at an outdoor table at a café on the Alameda waiting for Jenna to join them. Elena had asked Jenna to come hang out, but she and Alex really had more on the agenda.

"Hi, guys." Jenna smiled as she approached their table.

"Jenna." Alex beamed. "Hey, come have a seat."

Jenna pulled out one of the iron chairs as a waitress came to take their order.

"What's going on, guys?" Jenna asked, once the waitress left the table. "How's the casting going?"

Elena and Alex glanced at each other briefly.

"Actually, it's funny you ask." Elena let out a tight laugh. "We're having some trouble casting the female lead."

"You're not playing the lead, Elena?"

Elena shook her head. "I'm not playing anything."

Jenna looked puzzled.

"It's the way I want it. I'm going to direct and do other things, but I just don't belong anywhere on the stage."

"Well, I actually think you'd do a good job, but whatever. It's your play. I'm sure you guys know what's best."

The waitress delivered their drinks.

"So, what are you going to do about your leading lady?" Jenna asked.

"Actually, Jenna, we were thinking you would be an excellent leading lady," Alex said gently.

"What?" Jenna looked from Alex to Elena, then back to Alex.

Elena began to explain her theory on why Jenna was a born actress. "You're a natural performer, J. You dance up a storm every time we go out. You're inherently uninhibited. You have a great speaking voice. It's like the world is your stage."

"I don't know," Jenna said, scrunching her nose. "I've never acted before. Isn't there, like, a lot of memorization?"

"Jenna, I promise, if I can memorize all my lines, then you can, too." Alex laughed.

"Well, let me see the play." Jenna held out her hand, and Elena passed a copy of it across the table.

Jenna leafed through the first few pages. "So I'd be this Lisa person?"

Elena and Alex nodded.

"I don't know. I think I might be shy onstage."

"Jenna," Elena said, raising a skeptical eyebrow. "I can't believe you've ever been shy in your life."

"True. But I've never really been a performer either." Jenna was quiet for a while. "I'll have to have enough time to work on my final architecture project. And I won't be able to rehearse, or whatever, on Tuesday and Wednesday afternoons because that's when I'm getting together with my group for my final project."

"So, does that mean you'll do it?"

Jenna smiled. "Yeah. All right, I'll do it."

Alex leaned back in his chair and gave her a mock-serious look. "You know, Jenna, there's one thing we haven't told you about this role."

"What's that?"

"Well, I'm playing the main character, and at the end you would become my girlfriend...in the play."

"Hmm," Jenna leaned in toward the table with her chin

resting on her palm. She appeared to be giving Alex a seri-ous once-over. Then she leaned back again and said, "I think I can handle that."

"Okay, Jenna. You come on from stage left in this scene," Elena directed. They were only a week and a half away from their big performance. Elena had called all the actors together to rehearse some of their scenes for the last time before the dress rehearsal. Most of the actors were their friends and a couple of the better actors from class. An exceptional actress named Stephanie was playing the long-lost mother, Mrs. Walker. Chris, Marci, and Caitlin were playing strangers that the two main characters met along their journey. They had ten lines between the three of them. Even Alita had a role. She had begged Elena to let her play a part, so Elena had given her the role of Girl #2. Her one line was, "Mrs. Walker doesn't live here anymore," which she had insisted on repeating for Elena every night during dinner for the last week with a different inflection each time.

For the rest of the afternoon they would be working on an early scene in the play, where their two main characters, Jack and Lisa, meet each other and Jack convinces Lisa to help him find his mother. The scene involved only Jenna and Alex, so most of the other actors had already left the theater, but Alita stuck around to watch. Elena had been a little nervous about letting Alita hang around, fearing she'd dis-rupt everyone with her constant chattering, but so far she'd been very quiet and well behaved, sitting beside Elena in the audience and staring with saucer-big eyes at the older kids up on the stage. Elena couldn't help but feel a little proud, as though Alita were her real sister.

Jenna tried the scene again, but this time she fumbled two lines.

"Okay, you guys are really close to getting this," Elena said as she climbed the stairs on the side of the stage. "Jenna, you want to be more playful in your interaction with Alex's character. This girl doesn't take anything too seriously. They're flirting with each other, feeling each other out. Here, let me show you how I was thinking you could play it."

Elena took Jenna's place onstage.

"Come with me," Alex-as-Jack pleaded. "Help me look for my mom."

"My ex-boyfriend will be pissed," she said, trying to sound coy. "What do you need me for, anyway? You seem smart."

"I'm book smart. Do you know how far that gets me? About as far as the next corner, where I'll probably get mugged. Come on, you know this city. You told me you're streetwise, a drifter—this is right up your alley, so to speak."

"I told you I was a *free spirit*. There's a world of difference." Elena-as-Lisa raised an eyebrow. "Besides, I don't run off with strange boys."

"Neither do I," Alex returned in a perfect deadpan. "Come with me."

"What about my ex?"

"Hmm," Alex put his hand to his chin and smirked. "No, he can't come along."

Elena stopped the scene and looked at Jenna to see if she understood. Jenna sighed.

"You'll get it," Elena said. "No pressure."

"Okay I'll try it again." Jenna nodded, her face pulled into a studied frown. This was the first time Elena had seen Jenna go for more than a half hour without flirting or being silly. She was glad Jenna was taking this all so seriously. Elena resumed her seat next to Alita in the center of the audience.

As Alex and Jenna began the scene again, Elena heard someone jostling the seats in her row. She turned to find Ms. B scooting sideways along the row of seats. She settled into one of the squeaky seats beside Elena and smiled.

"How are rehearsals going?" she whispered to Elena, her eyes trained on the action unfolding onstage.

"Oh, they're good. We're just working out a few kinks."

"Mmm," Ms. B nodded, and watched in silence for a while.

"What are you doing here on a Saturday?" Elena asked.

"Oh, just catching up on some grading."

"You're checking up on us, aren't you? Making sure our play doesn't suck."

"It's possible." Ms. B laughed one of her big booming laughs, then clapped her hand over her mouth to keep from distracting the actors.

Elena made several notes of wrinkles in the stage direction that still needed to be ironed out.

"Okay, you guys, maybe we should take a break. Great job." Elena never realized putting on a play would require her to be writer, architect, choreographer, coach, and cheerleader. It was a big job, but she felt as if it suited her.

"We're going to run up to the store to get something to eat," Alex called from the stage.

"All right. Bring me back something, will you?" Elena hollered. Alita ran to join Jenna and Alex as they left.

"I have to say I'm a little surprised you didn't want the lead in your own play," Ms. B said.

"You're surprised?" Elena had figured Ms. B of all people would realize how shy she was. She never spoke up in class unless Ms. B called on her.

"Well, you know the material better than anyone."

"Ms. B, I'm really not outgoing at all. Jenna will do a much better job than I could. I'm just not one of those people who likes a lot of attention."

Ms. B held Elena's gaze and nodded slowly. She had a way of looking at kids to let them know she was really listening to what they said, even if she was about to try to change their minds.

"You know, Elena," she said after a long pause. "Acting is about a lot more than just standing up in front of people and saying, 'Look at me.'"

"I know."

"It's about inhabiting a character's psyche, being someone other than yourself." Ms. B was sitting forward in her seat, making big gestures that clinked her sliver bracelets together. "It's really the ultimate imaginative exercise. You have to become that other person. I just think someone like you, someone who is so creative and imaginative in her writing, might see acting as an extension of that creativity. Some of the best actors are introverts. I know it seems counterintuitive, but it's true."

"I guess it's just not my thing."

"Okay," Ms. B scooted back in her chair, looking a little deflated. "If you feel it's not for you, I understand."

One thing Elena was learning on this adventure in Spain was how to separate her dreams for herself from what other people wanted for her. She hated to let Ms. B down, but acting wasn't what she wanted for herself.

Ms. B looked as if she was about to say something else when Alex, Jenna, and Alita opened the door, letting a jarringly bright gash of sunlight into the darkened theater.

"We're back," Jenna called. "We got cheese, bread, and this fancy sausage from Pamplona."

"Yeah, we decided to have a picnic," Alita trilled.

Ms. B shifted in her seat and started to rise. "Well, I'll leave you to your picnic." Elena said good-bye and watched her walk out the door. Alita and Jenna were up on the stage spreading newspapers out to serve as a picnic blanket and unpacking the food. Elena headed toward the stage but was intercepted in the aisle by Alex. He tugged on her arm.

"Can I talk to you for a second?" he whispered.

"Sure."

"Outside."

"Okay." Elena nodded, though she couldn't understand why Alex was being so secretive.

"We'll be right back, you guys. Elena and I just have to run through some stage directions. Boring stuff," Alex called as he led Elena out the door.

"Are you sure she can do this?" he asked as soon as the door had shut behind them.

"Who? Jenna?" She was shocked he would even ask. "Of course she can do this."

"I don't know. She was pretty rattled all day."

"It's just because we're getting closer to the performance," Elena defended.

"Look, obviously I want her to stay in the play. I get to kiss her at the end—it would take a lot for me to give that up." He smiled for just a second, and then his face collapsed into seriousness again. "It's just that she seemed pretty conscious of who was watching her, and there were hardly any people in the theater. I'm nervous she might croak in front of a real audience."

"Relax. She's just getting the hang of it. It's only the

rehearsal—it's just a little bit of nerves. She'll be fine." Elena couldn't believe she was the one telling Alex to relax.

"I hope so. She's your best friend here—I'm sure you'd know if she couldn't handle the pressure."

"Exactly. Let's get back inside before all the food's gone."

They went back into the theater and joined the others onstage. Elena noticed that Alex slid right back into easy conversation with the group, but the wrinkle between his eyes betrayed a lingering anxiety.

Several days later, after deliberating with herself for hours, Elena finally gathered her courage and walked out into the main room of the apartment.

"I'm going to meet with Alex to work out some last-minute script changes," Elena called to the Cruzes as she headed out the door. Her little white lie made sense, since the final performance was now only two days away, but actually she wasn't meeting Alex until the following day. She was headed over to the garden outside the Maria Cristina.

Once she got there, she perched on a bench in the far corner of a section of grass. From her spot in the garden she could make out the entrance to the hotel without being seen. If she squinted, she could see Miguel's figure dashing in and out of the door, opening taxi and limousine doors, and giving every customer a little bow or a handshake.

She sat on the bench for twenty minutes. She didn't know

what she was waiting for. She knew that the longer she sat there, the more nervous she would get.

This was something she had to do. Elena was tired of living in her fantasies, she wanted something real. Even if it was a very real *rejection*, she owed it to her great-aunt Elena, to Alex, and to Jenna, and most of all herself to give it a try.

After a half hour at her post, Elena was biting her nails so short she was afraid her fingers might start to bleed. She decided to walk out toward the river, hoping the sight of water might calm her nerves. She made her way toward the Urumea River and walked along the back side of the hotel. Elena stopped for a moment, and glanced up. She searched for the balcony she'd stood on months ago with Miguel. It was the first time she had been close enough to smell his cologne, and the first time she'd been able to talk to him without stammering. She closed her eyes just for a moment and she could see it all perfectly. Miguel's face was etched on her brain.

"Elena?" She could see his face before she even opened her eyes. "What are you doing?" Miguel asked.

Okay, she could think of a reason why she was standing there with her eyes closed. It wasn't that weird. When she opened her mouth, nothing came out. *Smooth, Elena, very smooth.*

"Well, I was just helping José repair a guardrail, so I'm heading this way," he pointed in the direction of the main

entrance on the other side of the building. "Do you want to walk with me?" She nodded and fell into step with him.

"How are your play rehearsals going?" he asked after another moment of silence passed uncomfortably between them.

"They're good. We had one a few days ago, actually."

"And they went well?"

"Yeah. Everyone pretty much has their lines memorized now. We're just getting all the props together and making sure everyone knows which way to enter and exit."

Miguel nodded. "It sounds like a lot of work."

Just as Elena felt they were beginning to have a normal conversation, they approached the white-canopied entry to the hotel. Elena noticed for the first time that it was a humble entrance for such a grand hotel. The outside of the hotel was massive, but the real charm was on the inside.

"Well, I have to go talk to the manager, so I will see you later."

"Okay," Elena said. Her voice was hollow as she watched him turn to walk back inside. Her feet felt as if they were nailed in place. So this was it: She was just going to let him walk away? This was possibly her last opportunity to take some action on her own, to make something happen, and she just stood there watching it float away like a balloon caught on a swift breeze.

"Miguel, wait," she called, a little too loudly, chasing him down in the middle of the lobby. He turned to face her.

Elena wiped a sweaty palm on the front of her jeans and reached into her sweatshirt pocket, producing one shiny white ticket.

"I came here to give you this," she mumbled. "All the play-wrights get three tickets to give to people they want to come to the plays. We're supposed to give them to *special* people," her face burned when she said the word special. "I gave my other two to Señor and Señora Cruz," she added, holding the ticket gingerly out in front of her. "It would mean a lot to me if you came." She barely squeaked the last part out and felt as if she was slowly melting into the marble floor.

He looked up and began to say something when the manager called out to him. Miguel turned his head quickly, and a look of agitation washed over his face.

"Thank you," he said, taking the ticket from her hand. He hesitated for a moment and looked as if he might say more, but then turned toward the manager. Just before he sped off to the front desk, he slipped the ticket into the breast pocket of his shirt, right above his heart.

Chapter Thirteen

"I can't do this," Jenna whispered, her eyes shining under a thin veil of tears. "I mean, I really can't do this."

"What are you talking about, Jenna? You've been through this a million times."

"But never with all these people. It was always just you and me and Alex. I, I feel sick."

Elena pulled back the edge of one of the thick velvet curtains. The theater seats were sighing under the weight of so many audience members. She scanned the crowd searching for Miguel's face among the masses, but then let go of the velvet panel and let it fall back in place. She couldn't allow herself to look for him because if he was there it would make her even more nervous, and if he wasn't there, she was afraid she would be so disappointed that her heart might shatter into a thousand splintered pieces right there on the scuffed wood floor.

"Okay, Jenna. You can do this," Elena grasped her friend by the shoulders and looked into her eyes. "You can do this." She'd never believed in a statement so strongly, though she was starting to wonder if it was belief or denial.

"I can't, Elena. I've never performed in front of so many people."

What was she saying? Jenna wasn't afraid of anything. This was the girl who wanted to go topless her first day in San Sebastián. This was the girl who would dance all night in front of strangers; who didn't think twice about hitchhiking to Madrid. It wasn't possible that she was afraid of being onstage. Unless stage fright was her Achilles' heel, her kryptonite. Elena thought about the conversation she'd had with Alex about Jenna's possible stage fright after their rehearsal a week ago, but she quickly pushed it out of her mind.

"Okay everyone," Ms. B said. "Ten minutes to showtime."

Elena turned back just in time to see a green-faced Jenna clutching her mouth and streaking through the darkness toward the bathroom.

"Jenna's sick," Alex noted as he glided in beside Elena.

"Yeah, I think the whole theater can hear her."

"She's really freaking out about going onstage."

"She'll be fine," Elena said. She counted on Jenna to be the brave one.

"Look, Elena, you need a reality check. Jenna is really not fine, and we have to figure out what to do about it."

Elena chuckled and gave Alex a punch in the arm that was meant to be playful, but landed with a painful-sounding thud. "Jenna will come through. I believe that."

"You're freaking me out."

"Why? I'm totally calm."

"Exactly, that's why you're freaking me out. We're in deep here. You need to face it. Jenna's not going to be able to go on." Alex appeared on the verge of cracking. "Elena, we need a backup, and you are the only person who knows Jenna's lines and her stage directions as well as she does. Probably even better, actually."

Elena laughed. It was high-pitched and unnatural. "You're joking. I can't go out there. You think Jenna's a little freaked. I would have, like, a total meltdown. We need to find some-one else."

"There isn't anyone else."

Ms. B walked over to them with her clipboard in hand. "Are you guys all ready to go?" She started to run through the changing of the sets to make sure they had it down when Alex interrupted her and told her about their predicament.

"Well, that *is* bad news. Do you think she'll calm down enough to go on?"

Elena excused herself and ran over to the bathroom. She

stuck her nose into the crack between the door and the frame and called Jenna's name. The only response she heard was a groan. She tried the door, but it was locked.

"Jenna," she called. "Is everything all right in there? We're starting to get a little worried out here." She tittered. "Jenna?"

"I can't go out there, Elena."

"Jenna, you have to…."

"I can't do it."

Elena scurried back over to Ms. B and Alex. "Um, it might be a few minutes." She forced a cheerful smile.

"We have to go on in five," Alex practically screeched.

"Elena, you know I've always believed you would do a great job," Ms. B said gently, squeezing Elena's shoulder.

"Who says I'm going out there?" Now she was starting to lose her cool. "Jenna will be fine," Elena repeated for the third time in minutes. She was starting to sound like a delusional robot. Reality was beginning to sink in. She could feel the freak-out coming on like an earthquake.

"Elena," Ms. B grasped her shoulders gently and forced Elena to meet her eyes. "It would be a terrible shame if this play wasn't performed tonight. It deserves to be seen."

Something strange began to happen. The freak-out subsided. Elena heard herself say, "Okay, I'll do it. The show must go on, right?" Then she actually shrugged, as if what she was about to do was no big deal. As if standing up in front of a bunch of people and baring her soul was something she did every day. It was as if something had cracked

open inside her like an egg hatching. She had worked so hard on this play. It was her baby. She couldn't bear to see it die before it had even been given a chance.

The set movers scurried offstage, and Ms. B's voice floated through the theater announcing Alex and Elena's play. They were standing on the stage, just behind a line of shadow on the floor. As soon as they stepped into the light, they would find themselves out there in front of hundreds of people. Elena thought of the flamenco dancer in Madrid, the one who came out at the last minute and moved with such grace and ease. Her lack of rehearsal had made her appear that much more fresh and alive.

"You ready?" Alex whispered, squeezing Elena's hand.

"I'm ready," she said, and realized that she really meant it.

One of the acting techniques in dealing with stage fright Ms. B had taught the class was to imagine a fourth wall in place of the audience to make it seem as though they were really in an intimate setting. She told them to imagine a wall from a familiar, comforting place.

"Stage fright is really audience fright," Ms. B had lectured. "Your awareness of the fact that people are watching you is what will make you lock up. Get rid of the audience in your mind, and you'll get rid of the fear."

As soon as Elena found herself onstage she began to imagine the fourth wall. It wasn't as hard as she had thought because the lights were so intense that they threw the audience into blackness. It was like a blank canvas on which she painted a mental picture of one of the walls in her bedroom back home. She pictured the wall decorated with pages she and Gwen had ripped out of magazines. The wall was covered with black-and-white jewelry ads, photos of Johnny Depp and Josh Hartnett, pictures of models prancing through Parisian streets or rolling on the beaches of Brazil, pictures of horses and stilettos with heels cut like daggers. For a short time Elena was simultaneously in a theater in Spain, in her bedroom at home, and in this strange world she had created with Alex. Ms. B had been right; acting was the ultimate exercise in imagination.

Acts one and two went off so elegantly, Elena couldn't believe they were more than halfway through.

The mother-son reunion scene in the third act was one of the few where Elena didn't have to be onstage. She was able to stand backstage and watch the scene between Alex and Stephanie, who was playing his mother.

Alex and Stephanie sat facing each other on two prop chairs. The stage was set to look like a living room.

"You certainly were determined to find me," Stephanie said.

"Well, I was curious."

"About me or about yourself?"

"Both, I think," Alex said. He looked thoughtful. "I thought

that when I met you, it would be like looking in a mirror, that all the things I'd never really understood about myself would be reflected back at me in you."

"Well, I hate to disappoint you, Jack," Stephanie said in a gentle voice, "but I'm not a mirror."

"I know. I realized that just now. Even though this is the first time I've met you in my life, I feel like, in a way, I've always known you. It's something I feel..."

"In your heart," she said, finishing his thought.

Elena had added the last two lines of that scene on the train ride home from Barcelona. As she watched from behind the curtain offstage, she silently thanked her great-aunt Elena and her distant cousin Enrique for showing her that everything she needed to feel connected to her family, her heritage, was already inside her.

Elena took a deep breath and went back onstage for the final scene. They ended the play with Alex and Elena's characters getting together and kissing as the curtain dropped. Afterward, as she and Alex stood to take a bow in the hot center of the spotlight, she realized she had actually had fun. She liked pretending to be this person other than herself. She felt parts of herself she never knew were there opening up. Plus, the applause was dizzying.

The houselights came up a bit, and Elena could see familiar faces smiling, hands clapping wildly, and hear hoots and whistles rising up into the theater like a dust cloud.

Elena leaned in close to Alex and whispered, "We did it."

Alex smiled, grasped her hand, raised their interlocked arms, and led them into a swinging, dramatic bow.

"Your play was wonderful," Señora Cruz gushed.

Elena was glad the Cruzes were there to congratulate her on her performance. This was one of the times she really wished her family had been able to be with her. She knew her parents would have been so proud to see her up there. And Gwen would have been so happy to see Elena in the spotlight for once. On her way to Spain, Elena had hoped that in coming here she would surprise all of them with her bravery. On this night she would have blown them away.

"And you did a wonderful job with your part," Elena said to a beaming Alita. Señor Cruz patted Alita's head.

"We brought you these," Señora Cruz hollered over the din of the crowd buzzing past them. She handed Elena a bundle of white lilies wrapped in paper. As Elena was reaching out to hug the Cruzes, a pair of students interrupted.

"Great play," Gabe, Dylan's playwriting partner, said, pumping her hand formally as if she were in the receiving line at a wedding. Standing beside him was Dylan.

"We just wanted to tell you how awesome you were," Dylan said in a voice that managed to be cool and friendly at the same time.

"Thanks. You guys were great last night."

"Well, congratulations again," Dylan said as they turned to walk away. Their bodies were swallowed in the mass of people squashed into the cramped backstage area. Elena realized she hadn't even thought about Dylan since the day they'd chosen partners. She didn't have to be just like Dylan, or have her as a partner to be great. The whole idea seemed laughable now. She could be great just being Elena.

"Congratulations." Ms. B walked over and wrapped her arms around Elena. She gave her a squeeze. "Elena, I'm so proud of you for stepping in and saving the play. You must promise me you'll keep writing, acting, and directing."

Elena promised and accepted another hug from Ms. B.

"Where is Alex? I wanted to congratulate him, too."

"I don't know," Elena answered, scanning the crowd. They walked with the Cruzes through the backstage bustle. The entire playwriting class and all their friends were packed into the narrow corridor behind the stage that served as a mass dressing room. Elena and Ms. B waded through the crowd and found Alex standing along the wall hung with mirrors edged in round yellow bulbs. There were still-open makeup tubes and scattered powder brushes left idle in front of the mirrors. Alex was with Jenna, as well as Marci, Caitlin, and Chris. The only one missing from the group was Miguel. Elena felt her heart crack a little.

"Congratulations, Alex," Ms. B gushed, smothering him in a hug. Alex smiled and squirmed. He looked as uncomfortable as Elena in the face of all this sudden praise.

Jenna was standing in the center of the group—an impromptu theater-in-the-round—recounting her harrowing bout of stage fright. She was gesticulating wildly and had everyone laughing.

"Looks like you've gotten over your stage fright," Elena commented as she joined the circle. Jenna laughed and went in to hug Elena.

"You were awesome, Elena. I knew you could do a better job than me." Then she pulled Elena to the side and lowered her voice. "I'm so, so, so sorry I couldn't do it."

"You know what? It was fine. I'm happy about the way it worked out." Elena smiled, and she saw Jenna's shoulders relax.

"Really?"

"This was the way it was supposed to happen."

"Oh, like fate?" Jenna teased.

"Yeah, why not?"

Jenna gave her another big hug.

"So, you haven't seen Miguel around, have you?" Elena slipped the question in, hoping it sounded offhand.

Jenna shook her head. "I haven't seen him all night."

"Oh," she tried to keep the hurt out of her voice. She hadn't told Jenna about her special invitation for Miguel. In fact, she hadn't told anyone about it. It was just something she had wanted to keep to herself, and now she was glad she had because she didn't feel like sharing her disappointment with anyone. It was too raw.

Elena slumped forward, but she continued to scan the moving pack of people, looking for his face among them, in case Jenna was wrong. She even strained to search the corners bathed in shadow and thought she saw a figure standing in the darkness near the door. Alex approached her and broke her gaze.

"I'm taking off; I just wanted to say how awesome you were." Alex leaned in to give Elena a hug. He didn't give her a second to set down the flowers she was holding, and the paper made a crackling noise between them as Alex gave her a friendly squeeze.

Señor Cruz walked up and tapped Elena on the shoulder.

"Elena, we are going to leave soon. Would you like us to take you home?"

"Um, just a second." She peered over Señor Cruz's hair, combed slick with pomade, in another sweep for Miguel. She didn't want to think about what it would mean if he didn't show up.

Finally, she packed the little pieces of her heart, said her good-byes, and left without seeing Miguel. She went to bed that night wondering if it had all been a trick of her imagination, if Miguel's flirtations in Madrid and the encouragement from her friends had fooled her into thinking Miguel had feelings that didn't really exist.

Chapter Fourteen

Elena rolled up an old blanket she had borrowed from Señora Cruz. As she was stuffing it in her backpack she thought of her first day of Spanish class. It bothered her that she still hadn't become fluent in Spanish. She had yet to dream in Spanish the way Señor Gonzalez had told them they would once the language and the culture had become a part of them. She hated the idea that she might leave Spain tomorrow without taking a piece of it with her.

Tonight she and her friends were meeting at the beach at sunset. They were going to sleep under the stars listening to the waves and laughing together on their last night in Spain.

It had been Jenna's idea—a chance to bid farewell to San Sebastián and one another during one night.

Elena made her way toward the front door and spotted Alita on the couch, pondering a book for school. She'd been slumping around all evening and had barely uttered a word to Elena all day.

"*Hola,* Alita," she said, balancing on the arm of the couch and leaning over Alita's shoulder. Alita scooted away irritably. "What are you reading?"

"Nothing," Alita grumbled, her shoulders raised up toward her ears and her forehead pulled into a frown.

"Okay, well I'm going down to the shops to get some snacks for tonight. Do you want to come?"

Alita shook her head slowly. Now Elena was sure something was wrong. Alita, the girl who was always trying to tag along with whoever would tolerate her, was turning down an invitation. It wasn't like her at all.

"What's going on, Alita? You seem like you've been really down all day. Are you maybe upset because I'm leaving tomorrow?" Elena ventured. "You know, I'm going to keep in touch with you. We can e-mail and write each other postcards. And then maybe one day you can come and visit me in America." Elena said the last sentence in as perky a voice as she could muster. Alita nodded, the faintest wisp of a smile passed briefly on her lips.

Elena started to get off the couch when she heard Alita whisper something else. "What did you say?"

"I said I liked having a sister. I know you are not my real sister, but it was fun pretending. Now it will just be me."

"It's a little lonely, huh?"

"Yes," Alita nodded and finally set her book down. Elena sat down next to her on the couch cushion.

"Having brothers and sisters around can be a big pain, too. You compete over everything: the bathroom, the car, your parents' attention. Brothers tease. It's impossible to do anything really great because the chances are someone else has already done it, or can do it better than you...." As she was listing off all the downsides of having siblings, she realized how unconvinced Alita looked. She couldn't sell this to Alita because she didn't believe it herself. When she first arrived in Spain, she'd envied Alita. She knew Alita would always have her own room. She'd never have to follow in the footsteps of an impossibly beautiful sister. She'd never have to fight for her parents' attention. She'd never have to wear someone else's old, stretched-out clothes. Elena realized how little that mattered now. Elena didn't need to be away from her family anymore in order to do something really meaningful and big. In fact, now that she felt capable of doing those things, she wanted her siblings around to share them with her more than anything. They weren't her competition; they were her support system.

"I think I understand why you're sad. But you have some great friends, don't you?" Elena inquired.

"Yes." Alita slumped forward.

"Well, you don't have a big family, but your friends can be like extra family members you pick for yourself."

Alita nodded. She seemed to understand what Elena meant. Elena told Alita about her great-aunt Elena, who didn't have a husband and kids of her own but wasn't lonely because she surrounded herself with friends. Elena realized that she'd unwittingly done the same thing. She'd come to Spain to establish her independence, to set herself apart. But in the process she had surrounded herself with great friends whom she depended on, and she suspected they depended on her, too. It was a wonderful feeling.

"Well, you do have a sister for about sixteen more hours," Elena said, giving Alita's shoulders a squeeze. "Why don't you come with me to the store?"

Finally a smile broke out across Alita's stony face.

Hours after Elena had dropped Alita back off at home she was strolling along the Paseo toward the beach, and she spotted Miguel ambling toward her. The sun was at his back so that his face was hidden in shadow, but she was sure it was him. After months of scanning crowds for him she knew the real thing when she saw it. She had all of him memorized—his walk, his posture, the way he tipped his head to the side when he concentrated on something—all of him.

She'd been successful in avoiding him since the play. She didn't understand why he hadn't shown, and she was afraid she just didn't understand him, period. The fact that he hadn't shown up to the performance that meant so much to her was a sign that he was truly not interested. So she had avoided him to prove that she wasn't interested either.

Elena ducked her head and tried to dart over to the stairs before he could see her, but he was too quick.

"Elena," he called. He picked up his pace and met her in front of the steps.

Elena spotted her friends—a line of shadowy figures filing across the sand. "I'm supposed to be meeting them," she said, pointing to the moving silhouettes.

Miguel looked in the direction she pointed, then they both looked at each other.

"I know. Jenna told me. That's how I knew you would be here." So, he had been looking for her. Neither of them moved. She looked back toward her friends in the distance.

"I was hoping I could talk to you," he said.

"Okay." Elena couldn't stop her mind from racing. What could he possibly have to say to her on her last night there?

"Come with me," Miguel said, reaching gently for her hand and leading her toward an empty bench overlooking the ocean. His face was turned away from the sun, but his eyes still seemed to reflect strands of gold.

They sat in silence for a moment, watching the setting sun dance across the water. The fact that she was actually leaving tomorrow hadn't seemed real until that moment as she realized this would be her last sunset in San Sebastián.

Elena closed her eyes and tried to save the view just as

she saw it now with the sun dropping quietly into the ocean.

"Sometimes, when I come to watch the sun go down, I can see the moment when the horizon flashes green just before darkness," Miguel said. Was this his way of trying to patch things up before she left forever, she wondered.

"I've never seen the green flash." Elena nodded, intrigued. "It sounds beautiful."

"It is." He was quiet again and looked straight ahead, but she sensed he had more to say. She waited a long time as the wind picked up off the ocean and the air grew cooler.

"I went to your play," he said finally. "It was wonderful."

"You came? But I never saw you. No one did."

"I was there," he assured her.

"But nobody saw you. Why didn't you—"

"I was there," he barreled through, interrupting her thought. "I was called in at the last minute for work, and I got off only ten minutes before your play started, so I had to sneak in and sit in the back, but I was there. I was also backstage after the show. I brought flowers for you. They were the same kind you were already holding—the ones that Alex had given you."

"Alex?" she turned abruptly to face him. "Those flowers weren't from Alex; they were from the Cruzes."

"But you were hugging him and smiling."

"We had just finished a really difficult project together. He's just my friend."

Miguel looked down at his hands. "I did not know that. I

thought you might be with him. You had been spending so much time with him. And then you kissed each other onstage. I was sitting in the audience wondering why you had asked me to come and watch you kiss another boy."

Elena couldn't help but laugh. She forced him to look her in the eyes. "First of all, Alex has always been just a friend. Second, we were acting. It's all pretend. And I wasn't even the one who was supposed to be kissing Alex at the end of the play, Jenna was." Elena felt herself relaxing. She was so happy and relieved that Miguel had hunted her down to tell her he had been at the play after all. "Jenna was our lead. She was supposed to play the main character, Lisa, but she got really nervous that night. Right before we went onstage, she panicked, and I had to step in for her."

"That was brave."

Elena looked out at the ocean and mumbled a thank-you. She didn't tell him how much more courage it took her just to ask him to the play. Starring in a play had seemed like nothing compared to the nerves she felt standing at the hotel, practically handing her heart to Miguel. "Believe me, if I had known I was going to be the one up there kissing Alex at the end, I would have at least warned you."

"Well, I'm glad to hear that, Elena, because...I like you," he said to his hands. "I wanted you to know that."

Elena couldn't believe what she was hearing. Miguel—the person she thought was too beautiful and confident ever to care for her—was sitting here saying he felt the same way

about her that she had felt about him all this time. Elena looked at his profile, haloed by the light of the sunset. It was the way she had first seen him, in a profile that was practically glowing. Then she glanced back at the ocean.

The sun was just a point of yellow light on the waves; she could see it slipping slowly, slowly into the water.

She wanted to thank him for finding her on her last night and to tell him that this would be a moment she'd remember for years. But the words never left her mouth. Miguel leaned in, took her face in his hands, and kissed her just as the sun slipped into the ocean in a fleeting, brilliant flash of green.

Miguel and Elena found their group on the beach up near the Paseo. As they approached, they found Alex fumbling with big hunks of wood and frighteningly long matches, attempting to start a bonfire in the dark. He claimed it was a necessary skill for any respectable beach bum.

Jenna waved them over excitedly. "Hi, you guys," she said, leaping up to give them both tight hugs.

Elena plunked down in the sand with Jenna and unloaded the proliferation of junk food she'd been lugging around in her backpack with the blankets. She knew she'd gone overboard, and she knew all the girls would complain about their caloric intake and then stuff their faces anyway.

"Elena, why did you get so much junk?" Marci whined as she reached for a package of cookies and tore it open.

"You know you love it, Marci," Jenna teased, reaching for a bag of chips.

Alex finally got the bonfire started. Miguel moved in next to Elena, wrapping his arm around her waist and pulling her onto his lap. Chris turned on a little battery-powered radio he'd brought along and tinny flamenco music came pumping through the rusted speakers. The music was scratchy and weak, but Alex and Jenna got up and did a little impromptu flamenco routine. Elena was happy to see that Jenna had eventually given in to her obvious feelings for Alex. Although she knew they were both so noncommittal it probably wouldn't go anywhere beyond that night, she was happy to see her two best friends together for now.

Eventually Jenna persuaded Chris, Marci, and Caitlin to get up and join the dance party.

Elena stayed firmly planted, leaning back against Miguel, with his arms wrapped securely around her waist. Now that she was with him she didn't want to let go. This wasn't just another one of her daydreams. This was the real thing. This was an actual guy with insecurities and faults and dreams of his own. She turned her head and kissed him again.

The plan had been to stay up talking and goofing around until dawn when they would all watch the sunrise together from their spot on the beach. During his time in San Sebastián, Alex had been up before dawn several times in order to get a couple of good hours of surfing in before

school, and he promised them that dawn breaking over la Playa de la Concha was a magical sight. But around three in the morning, some members of the group were fading. Marci and Caitlin were the first to go, followed by Chris, who ended up falling asleep with his face mashed into the sand. Jenna and Elena had to gently shove a balled-up jacket under his head so he wouldn't wake up with sand in his mouth. Then, Jenna fell asleep on Alex's chest.

Miguel and Elena lay together on Señora Cruz's blanket and looked up at the stars.

That night Elena had a week's worth of dreams. She had strange dreams about getting on a ship with Miguel, Jenna, and Alex, and yet somehow watching them float away. She dreamed of her family and Claire waiting for her back home, and how it would feel to hug them all at the airport. She had dreams about getting stuck in a plane circling over Spain and the United States, unsure where to land. She dreamed of the beach and trains and finely dressed Spanish men sitting at outdoor cafés.

Miguel woke her in time to see the light of dawn spreading pink across the sky. She sat up in the sand and looked at all her other friends still asleep on the sand. Although she wouldn't remember any of the details of her dreams that night under the Spanish sky, she knew that the whole time she had been dreaming in Spanish.